SECONDS TO LIVE

I was alone in the basement dumping a load into the trash compactor. As I did, I heard the sound of bottles clinking against each other, and I had to climb into the damn thing until I found them.

Then suddenly I heard a noise. Whoever was out there was standing right next to the front of the machine. Then I heard a sharp sound—Click!—followed immediately by the earsplitting roar and screech of the huge steel compactor lid moving toward me. I was shaking and screaming. I lost all control, ran around blindly, slammed into the walls, bounced off, screamed at the top of my lungs.

I started crying then, really crying, knowing I had only seconds left . . .

Other Avon Books by
John Minahan

9/30/55

EYEWITNESS

Based on a Screenplay written by Steve Tesich

John Minahan

AVON
PUBLISHERS OF BARD, CAMELOT AND DISCUS BOOKS

EYEWITNESS is an original publication of Avon Books. This work has never before appeared in book form.

Grateful acknowledgment is made to New Directions Publishing Corporation for permission to quote from THE NIGHT OF THE IGUANA by Tennessee Williams, Copyright © 1961 by Two River Enterprises, Inc. Reprinted by permission of New Directions.

AVON BOOKS
A division of
The Hearst Corporation
959 Eighth Avenue
New York, New York 10019

Published by arrangement with Twentieth Century-Fox Film Corporation
Library of Congress Catalog Card Number: 80-68428
ISBN: 0-380-77388-0

First Avon Printing, March, 1981

AVON TRADEMARK REG. U.S. PAT. OFF. AND IN OTHER COUNTRIES, MARCA REGISTRADA, HECHO EN U.S.A.

Printed in the U.S.A.

For

PHYLLIS HILL,

a patient eyewitness to
understanding and love.

My conclusions have cost me some labor from the want of coincidence between accounts of the same occurrences by different eyewitnesses.

—Thucydides
c. 460-400 B.C.

EYEWITNESS

1

THE SUMMER IT HAPPENED, I'd just turned thirty and I was a janitor working the night shift in the old Waring Building down at Sixth Avenue and Forty-first Street. That's just across the street from Bryant Park, you know, behind the New York Public Library? Not a bad area, but not good either. Some of the guys who worked the day shift in the building called themselves maintenance engineers, but I never went in for shit like that. We were janitors. We cleaned up the trash from the offices and washed and buffed the floors and did simple repair work, you know? What's so bad about that? I'll tell you the truth, I was never ashamed of being a janitor. It was honest work, it was quiet on my shift, and I was pretty much my own boss. I was an ex-Marine, I'd served in Vietnam, and I'd tried a lot of other jobs when I got out. Couldn't hack them. Couldn't settle down for a while. This buddy of mine, Allan Mercer, everybody calls him Aldo, we met in the service and we used to talk about opening up our own sporting goods store when we got back home. We used to talk about it all the time. We knew the area we wanted in Manhattan, the Upper West Side near Columbia, we knew the start-up operating capital we'd need, we made lists of the inventory, our wholesale and retail costs, the whole nine yards. Sometimes, when things got rough over there, that dream kept us going.

We were both into sports when we were kids, we both wanted to be ballplayers. That was my ambition when I was in high school, to be a professional baseball player. I'd reached my full height in my senior year, six feet two,

I was an outfielder and a pretty fair hitter. In fact, I was a damn good hitter, modesty aside. I had the four essential abilities that Leo Durocher always mentioned: I could hit, hit with power, run and throw. But not good enough to land a contract. Same with Aldo, except he was a catcher. So, what can I tell you? Those dreams went down the drain.

Anyway, we both got back from Vietnam the same year, 1972. I was twenty-two, Aldo was twenty-one, and we really thought we had the world by the ass on a downhill drag. I mean, you do at that age, right? We thought we had an excellent shot at the sporting goods store through a loan from the Small Business Administration. Instead of opening up from scratch, we were looking to buy out some established little store, inventory and all, take over the lease, and set ourselves up immediately, just the two of us. A small place to start with, nothing fancy, no big overhead. We'd undercut competitive prices and make up the difference in volume sales. While we were waiting for our loan to be approved, we even began scouting locations on the Upper West Side. You'll be surprised how relatively few good sporting goods stores are up there from, say, Amsterdam to West End, Eighty-sixth to 114th. It was exciting to look them over, to imagine the possibilities. God, we were really excited about it.

Well, to make a long story short, we had trouble getting the small-business loan. No previous business experience, not nearly enough collateral security, and my father wouldn't cosign the note for us. No way. He's a great guy and I love him, but he's a hard-core realist. In his words, the whole idea was "complete pie-in-the-sky bullshit." That's exactly how he felt. That's more or less how my mother felt, too, although she never actually said so.

What they really wanted, what they'd wanted all along, was for me to get a college education on the G.I. Bill, and their arguments were very persuasive. I was still young enough, but after Vietnam I just couldn't see myself sitting in classrooms with kids. So I lived at home for about a year, tried a total of four different jobs, and none of them lasted more than a few months. Each time I'd leave a job, Mother and Dad would apply pressure about college again. Well, my grades in high school had been above average, despite the fact that it bored the piss out of me, so I finally applied to the School of General Studies at Columbia. I swear to God, I didn't really believe I'd get in. But I did. I was accepted for the fall term, 1974, as a "non-degree candidate" (that's like probation), and I resigned myself to give it a try. I lasted exactly two years, that's all I could stand, but when I dropped out I was a full-fledged degree candidate, an English major, so I didn't do too badly. Also, I discovered something about myself. I found out I had some degree of talent for writing.

That was fine, but, as my father pointed out: (a) English majors are axiomatically qualified for precisely nothing, particularly without a degree, and (b) if I had any illusions about getting into journalism, I'd selected probably the worst moment in the history of the country. Ever since Bernstein and Woodward had broken the story on Watergate in 1972, and published *All the President's Men* in 1974, investigative reporting had become the hottest career goal of the decade; all the graduate schools of journalism around the country had been absolutely swamped with new students, who were now graduating and flooding the job market to such an unbelievable extent that papers like *The New York Times* and the Washington *Post* actually had Ph.D. degree-holders in journalism on the waiting list for jobs as copy boys!

That was the spring of 1976. Well, I lived at home for another year, tried a number of jobs again, about five this time, as I remember it, and finally lucked into the one in the Waring Building, the janitor's job. My father wasn't too thrilled about it, to say the least—"my son the janitor"—but I liked it. It gave me time to step back and breathe, if you know what I mean.

After the first seven months on the job, I moved out of my parents' house and got an apartment of my own down on West Fourth Street in Manhattan. Then, after I'd been on the job about two years, one of the guys on the night shift quit. Now, I'd been telling Aldo about my job, about how hassle-free it was, the hours, the pay, and how I really felt comfortable for the first time, right? Well, he envied me that, because he really hated his job. He was working in the mailroom at CIT up at 650 Madison, one of about half a dozen jobs he'd bounced around in since we got out in '72. Every job he had, same story, some dip-shit supervisor was like looking over his shoulder, giving him a hard time. I knew what that was like. All the times it happened to me, I'd take it for a while, then I'd just quit. Aldo, his temperament was very different from mine. I mean, he'd give the guy an argument, you know? On two jobs he had, I think it was the first two, he actually slugged some clown. Of the six or seven jobs he had, he'd been fired from four. So he'd gone the unemployment route at least four times, and he didn't like that either, standing in line and all, answering questions, kissing ass to get his unemployment check. He was something, Aldo.

Anyway, I told him about this opening on the night shift. In fact, I called him the minute I found out and told him to get his ass in gear and go see the real estate agent fast, and that I'd back him up, vouch for him and all. Well, he got really excited and got his act together and went down and saw the people and applied for the job. He put me down for a reference and I was asked to write a letter of recommendation. I did, and then I brought it into the office myself and laid it on a little thick about his character and honesty, all shit like that, but I tried not to overkill, okay? The bottom line, he got the job. Night shift, my shift. He was laughing and shouting on the phone, he couldn't believe it. I remember the exact date, Wednesday, May 7, 1980. We decided to celebrate that night.

My hours were from five in the afternoon to one in the morning, so we agreed to meet at O'Henry's at about one-thirty, or just as soon as I could get there. I was really excited that night. I finished up a little early, showered, changed fast, locked up the building, and—ready for this?—jumped on my motorcycle. Yeah! It was a BMW B75/61 enduro-type cycle, one of the very few "luxury" things I owned, and I really dug that bike, it gave me a lot of joy, you know? To come out of that building, feeling fresh from a shower, put on my helmet, rev the engine, then blast away on that mother? You kidding? Beats the hell out of the subway, right? That time of morning was beautiful, very little traffic. I usually tooled east on Forty-second, hung a right on Fifth, which is one-way south-bound, and had a nice clear shot all the way to Washington Square Park. Not speeding, just judging the traffic lights right. That cycle was a kick in the ass. Loved it!

When I got to O'Henry's, Aldo was already there at a window table in the bar area with a big pitcher of beer and two mugs, raring to go. A lot of Village people think O'Henry's has turned into a tourist trap, and I guess it does in the summer, but Aldo and I liked it. It was an old steak house on the corner of Sixth Avenue and West Fourth, near my apartment and within easy driving distance of his. It was expensive to eat there, but you could have a couple of pitchers of beer and get off pretty light, plus the atmosphere was nice and informal, sawdust on the floor, checkered tablecloths, big Casablanca-type ceiling fans and like that. It was fairly warm that night, and a lot of people were sitting at the tables outside—O'Henry's had a little sidewalk café type of deal in warm weather—but Aldo and I didn't like it out there because you got hassled by bums and junkies and stuff.

One thing about Aldo, he was a good dresser. Made a nice impression. Had a lot of sport coats, shirts, ties, slacks, inexpensive but fashionable. That night he wore a light-blue polyester shirt, form-fitting, and dark-blue cords. Doesn't sound like much, but on him it looked good. The only way I can think of to describe Aldo, he looked like a catcher. If you know baseball, you know exactly what I mean. He was built like a catcher, he moved like one, he acted like one, he even had the hands. I used to tell him he was Johnny Bench City. He was, too, except he had more hair.

We rapped for a while, talked about the new job, then I told him something I knew he'd find out sooner or later. Better sooner. I waited until we were into the third mug of beer.

"Remember Mr. Long in Saigon?"

He hesitated, frowned. "Long. Mr. Long."

"We didn't actually know him, we knew *of* him."

"You mean the pusher, the hustler, the old guy?"

"That's him. Chauffeured around in that broken-down old—"

"Oh, yeah, now I remember. That old—what was it, a Packard?"

"Packard, right, that was it. Big whitewall tires and all?"

He laughed. "Yeah, sold shit to both sides, didn't he? Sold anything to anybody who had the price."

"Pot, coke, heroin, whores. Troop movements, anything."

"Heard he was even spying for the Russians."

"That was the rumor. Spying on his own allies."

Aldo sipped his beer, smiled, looked out the window. "Christ, I haven't thought about that old Packard in—how long we been back? Eight years?"

"Ever wonder what happened to him?"

"Mr. Long? Shit. Probably retired a millionaire."

I lit a cigarette. "He got out."

"Out of Nam? Where to?"

"He was in Cambodia in April, 'seventy-five. Remember reading about that emergency helicopter evacuation in Phnom Penh? On the eve of the takeover by the Khmer Rouge?"

"Saw it on the news, yeah."

"It was our choppers, four Marine choppers. Evacuated I think it was like four hundred and seventy people. Handful of Cambodians and the rest Americans. Included Ambassador Dean and his staff. And a shitload of journalists, about forty or fifty journalists."

"What, Long got out that way?"

"Passed himself off as a Cambodian. Paid people off."

He shook his head. "Where'd he end up?"

"New York. Opened up a new business here."

"No shit! *Here?* Doing what?"

"Long and Son. Import-export. Diamonds."

"Son of a bitch." He lit a cigarette, inhaled deeply, blinked at me through the smoke. "So how come you know all this?"

"He's in our building, Aldo. He's got an office in the Waring Building. Second floor, front. Long and Son. Import-export."

I remember how his eyes narrowed and crinkled just before he pursed his lips and nodded slowly. That's why he made a lousy poker player. "I got it, Daryll. I got it. He took one look at you, blond hair, blue eyes, gold-framed glasses, scholarly, clean-cut, Irish, ex-Marine, right? He's negotiating with you to become—or maybe you already closed the deal. Let me take a guess. A courier. Right?

Perfect. Perfect cover. You empty his baskets every night, pick up the cash, diamonds, whatever. Little by little."

"Aldo."

"Friday nights, you're into the dark three-piece suit, off to JFK, night flight to—Switzerland? Got to be Switzerland."

"Aldo."

"No, huh? Okay, he promised you a diamond for Linda, right? Two carats, minimum, for the engagement ring. All you got to do is play it D and D. And more where that came from."

"Aldo."

"No, huh?"

"I'm serious. I know it sounds crazy, but I'm telling you. I didn't—the first time I saw the name on the door, it never even—I didn't even give it a second thought. The first time I saw Long and his son inside, it didn't even register then. What really did it, about eight or nine months ago, I was coming to work, I saw them leave in a limo. A chauffeured black Caddy limo. That triggered it. Then I started asking around. It's him. No question. I swear to God."

Aldo nodded, shrugged, sipped his beer, glanced out the window, let it sink in. Then: "So what? Who the hell cares?"

"I just wanted you to know."

"What, you think I'd hold a grudge or what?"

"No. Not at all. Just wanted to clue you in before you start the new job, that's all. Don't want anything bugging you."

"Okay. Appreciate it."

"So, you start Monday, right?"

"Monday night, right."

"You give CIT your notice today?"

"No, I'll quit Friday. Screw them, I don't owe them nothing."

"You'll like this job. I guarantee it."

He finished his beer, poured another. "Tell me something up front. You think I'd let a scumbag like Long get on my tits?"

"No way. I told you."

"Daryll, that's—ancient history as far as I'm concerned. I mean it. Who the hell cares about people like him?"

"Not me. I couldn't care less. Just didn't want you to find out from somebody else. We're buddies, right? That's what it's all about. We think about the other guy. We anticipate, okay?"

"Right. Let's drop the subject right there. Come on, finish up, we'll get another pitcher. We're supposed to be celebrating here."

It went like that. We ordered another pitcher of beer and began toasting to the future and started to feel really good. Then we got on our favorite subject, the sporting goods store. Now that we'd both have steady jobs and both be making pretty good money, we could settle down and do a lot more maneuvering. I told him the progress I'd made on a new scheme to raise some front money, a writing project that I'll explain in detail later on, and Aldo brought me up to date on some contacts he'd made who might actually be interested in loaning some heavy bread if we could manage the finance changes, which were unusually high. See, you have to understand, we'd just never given up on that dream. It would cool occasionally, of course, sometimes we wouldn't discuss it for weeks at a time, but it was always there. It was always alive. It was the future. It was something special to shoot for. It was something to think about when you woke up and didn't really feel like going to work. By that time it was getting to be an obsession with us. It was one dream that was absolutely, positively going to happen, no matter how long it took, no matter what we had to do, no matter what, period. You know that feeling?

Well, we left O'Henry's about two-thirty, as I remember it, because Aldo had to go to work in the morning, he couldn't afford not to. We weren't exactly drunk, but we were feeling no pain, I'll tell you. He got on the back of my cycle and I drove him home slowly, just took East Fourth to Broadway, then to Canal Street, hung a left, then a right on Mott. He lived in a little dump on Bayard, near Confucius Square, smack in the middle of Chinatown.

I'd been dating his sister, Linda, who was nineteen, for about a year then. She worked days as a cutter in a small theatrical wardrobe manufacturing shop on West Forty-third, went to NYU nights, and lived on West Tenth, within walking distance of my place. She was a little young for me, but she was a dynamite girl, bright, fun to be with, and we had a lot in common. Aldo was really tickled that we'd hit it off, because he felt responsible for her. Both their parents were dead.

Driving back to my apartment that night, I couldn't help thinking how he'd reacted to my information about Mr. Long. He'd said all the things he knew I wanted to hear, but when you get to know a guy as well as I knew Aldo, inside and out, you listen to other things.

You listen to what a guy doesn't say.

2

EVERYBODY HAS FANTASIES, I guess, and I'm no exception. After I drove Aldo home that night, I went back to my apartment and looked forward to a kind of fantasy I'd been having for around six months. I lived in a nice old converted brownstone, second floor of a five-story former townhouse on West Fourth, just a small one-bedroom bachelor-pad type of deal, but a big chunk of my salary went into rent. I had a beautiful German shepherd named Ralph, who I'd bought as a puppy when I was still living with my parents, and he gave me a lot of joy every day. Since I worked nights and had to be a night person, Ralph had learned to be a night dog. For example, on a typical weeknight, I'd get home about one-thirty or so, play with Ralph, watch television, have dinner (Ralph, too) at maybe two or two-thirty, take Ralph for his walk, then come back and read or watch TV till about six o'clock or so, when we usually turned in. Wonder what I watched on TV that late? Think nothing good is on in the wee hours? Wrong. I saw all the prime-time shows, local and network news, the whole nine yards, thanks to my Sony four-hour video cassette recorder. Cost a bundle, had to buy it on a twenty-four-month installment plan, but it was worth every nickel. A lot of night people have them these days. If you enjoy watching TV, you don't have much choice. Next to my cycle, it was the most expensive thing I had.

My landlady, Helen Curry, a real sweetheart of a woman who lived upstairs, had an agreement with me to come down to my apartment every weeknight about seven o'clock and turn on my video cassette. In return, I promised to keep the volume at a very normal level, which in my case was relatively low. Anyway, I could come home every night and watch all the shows that ran from about seven to eleven, okay? Now, after dropping Aldo off that night, I got home about three o'clock or so, looking forward to my fantasy, but first I had to go through my usual routine with Ralph. What I did, I'd make a little extra noise when I was unlocking my door, so Ralph would have time to hide.

I went in, snapped on the light, paused as I shut the door, listening, then turned and glanced around cautiously. Silence. I stood very still, listening, then took a careful step forward and—*wham!*—Ralph leaped out at me from nowhere, knocked me sideways, growling viciously, and we were on the floor in a flash, wrestling. People who saw our bit for the first time were absolutely terrified. Over the years, we'd polished it into a class act, a believable attack. It never lasted more than thirty seconds or so, but that night I cut it very short because I was a little tired. I just told Ralph: "No more." Like most dogs, he responded best to very short commands. He stopped immediately, licked my face, and made the little sounds in his throat to say he was happy to see me. Then he followed me into the kitchen, wagging his tail. I got a can of Bud from the refrigerator, went in the living room, turned on the TV, pressed the rewind button on the video cassette and watched the ten-o'clock news in fast reverse with the volume turned down all the way. I was only interested in the last hour of the tape, the news, so I watched the rewind until the approximate middle of the show, the sports segment. When that appeared, I stopped the tape, pressed the forward button, turned the volume up to normal, and sat on the couch. Ralph put his head on my lap.

I wasn't particularly interested in the sports segment that night, I was anxious to begin my fantasy, so I just sipped my beer and waited. Finally, the anchorman introduced the drama critic, Tony Sokolow, and the instant she appeared on the screen, it began to happen all over again. I sat forward and just stared.

How can I explain this? I've never tried before, but I'll give it a shot. I suppose the feeling I had for her, the intense emotional reaction that had been going on for six months, was some kind of complicated psychological chemistry, the recognition of a need never before experienced. Let me begin with the tangible: Tony Sokolow was a young Jewish girl with facial characteristics that just missed being aristocratic, thank God, in favor of an almost subliminal earthiness. Her oval face was framed by thick dark hair worn shoulder-length, and her dark-brown eyes looked directly at the camera, directly at you, wide, bright, unwavering. I suppose she wore mascara, but there was no trace of lipstick, her mouth had good definition, and the chin was very firm. She was thin as opposed to slim and her fashion signature was simplicity. If anything dominated her personality on camera, it had to be her voice. It fluctuated on a kind of musical scale from the contralto of conviction and persuasiveness to the slightly higher chords of sarcasm and anger to the occasional soprano of humor, but the tone was always conversational, as if she were speaking to one person only, you, in a relaxed vernacular, in your living room, explaining something of genuine interest to you, something important, wanting you to understand, wanting you to care.

Tony wasn't a "regular" on the local news team; that is, she normally appeared only on weekends, but she substituted for the regular drama critic, Terry Randall (who was a pompous dilettante asshole), on weeknights when he was on special assignment or ill or on vacation. She also pinch-hit for other regulars on the news staff, and I'd seen her report on subjects ranging from movies and music to politics and crime.

There are few, if any, Broadway openings on weekends, so Tony usually had the option of rehashing what Randall had already said about the plays that opened during the week or making highly personal commentaries about directors, producers, playwrights, actors, actresses, or the state of the theater in general. But that night she'd attended the opening of a new musical, so it was an unusual opportunity for her. I liked her review so much that I ran the video cassette back, played it again, and recorded the audio on my tape recorder. Here's a verbatim transcription:

The musical is called *Robin*—Robin being Robin Hood—and if you think the Knicks are incompetent, you should see these merry men flitting across the Shubert-owned Sherwood Forest with their bows.

In the great tradition of taking from the rich and giving to the poor, the producers of *Robin* did likewise. They took from their rich backers and gave to the poor. The poor in this case are the lyricist, very poor; the book writer, extremely poor; and, the poorest of them all, the composer.

The cast, like the Sherwood Forest, was made of solid cardboard. Friar Tuck should have been roasted. And Robin, the merriest of them all, or gayest, seemed only to come to life when Maid Marian left and Little John came on. Their duet, "Me and My Bow," is a classic.

The orchestra wisely stayed in the pits, where the whole show belonged.

That's what Tony said, and she never even raised her voice above a conversational tone, as usual. She was like that. She said what she really felt. You could see it in her eyes, you could hear it in her voice. She didn't want to play games with people. She just went ahead and said it all out, exactly what she believed, as honestly and calmly as she could express it.

Well, that's my best shot at explaining how I reacted to Tony. It was like an awakening for me. She seemed to have exactly the right combinations of exactly the right emotional, psychological and physical qualities in a woman that I'd sort of daydreamed about for years. I knew she was single (no ring), that she was probably dating the cream of the crop around New York, and I understood intuitively that she wouldn't look twice at a clown like me.

Still, I needed her. Not somebody like her, because there wasn't anybody like her. I needed her, the genuine article, I wanted her, I thought about her all the time, every day for those six months. So, the only way I can explain what happened, I suppose my mind just finally compensated for the need, at least temporarily: illusion for reality. Which was an immensely pleasant sensation, because I just didn't like many of the realities of my life back then.

I began fantasizing that Tony Sokolow and I lived together, that we were lovers. It got to be an elaborate thing and I don't want to go into the intimate part of it here, but you can probably imagine all that, right? We both worked nights, so that was perfect. During the week, we'd both get home around the same time, have drinks, shoot the breeze, relax, watch the news, have dinner. Take Ralph for his walk together, come back, maybe catch some more TV on her channel, see the ten-o'clock news, boo Terry Randall, then go to bed and make love—almost every night at first.

Then, on weekends, we'd spend part of the day together and she'd have to go off to the studio fairly early to prepare. Okay, since I was dating Linda almost every weekend, that worked out fine. I could make the transition because I fantasized that Tony knew all about Linda, had met her and all, liked her, and encouraged me to go out with her on weekend nights when she had to work. In reality, I liked Linda a lot. We'd been friends since Aldo introduced us in 1972, when she was eleven and I was twenty-two. When she was eighteen and we started dating, before Tony came into the picture, I even thought I might be in love with her, and I think she felt the same. The fact is, our age difference was actually starting to get in the way, despite all the things we had in common, and we both knew that. I'm sure she noticed the change in me after I started the fantasy about Tony. Maybe I should've tried to explain it to her. She was just kooky enough to understand where my head was, and we probably could've worked it out. But the truth is, I didn't want to work it out. I didn't want reality.

During the six months that I studied Tony, she gradually began to change my life in the world of reality. I found that my thinking started to be channeled into areas that were relatively new to me. My reading preferences changed, not only in books, but in newspapers and magazines. My value judgments began to be subtly altered. For example, one weekend Tony did a commentary on an off-Broadway revival of Tennessee Williams's *The Night of the Iguana,* and I realized for the first time how deeply she cared about the man and his work. I didn't know a hell of a lot about Tennessee Williams before that night; I'd never even seen one of his plays. I mean, I'd seen some of the films that were adapted from the plays, mostly on television, like *Cat on a Hot Tin Roof* and *The Rose Tattoo* and *A Streetcar Named Desire,* stuff like that, but I think I was more interested in the stories and the stars than in Williams. The fact that Tony was really moved by the guy fascinated me to the point where I wanted to find out a lot more about the man, fast. That became a high priority immediately.

Anyway, the day after her commentary, before I went to work, I drove up to the Drama Book Shop on West Fifty-second and spent more than an hour in there looking through all of Williams's published plays (they had twenty-four of them), his short story collections, his two novels, his book of poetry, even his autobiography. They also had tons of books *about* him, but I wanted stuff *by* him. I didn't have that much money on me, so I wasn't sure which books to get, except, of course, *The Night of the Iguana.* Because of what Tony had said about the last lines in that play, how they made her cry, I'd grabbed that book first, as soon as I entered the store and found the Williams section, and I'd turned to the last page fast and read the lines three or four times. And, in the context of what she'd said about that play being Williams's last commercial success, I understood only too well.

Well, I explained to the salesperson that I only had a little money on me and asked what she recommended by Williams. She was obviously into the guy too, because she didn't hesitate, just smiled and said, *"Menagerie, Streetcar, Cat, Sweet Bird,* and *Iguana."* I was really glad she included *Iguana.* I bought all five and walked out of that bookstore feeling just a little closer to Tony.

Although I was very tempted to start reading *Iguana* during my lunch break, I wanted to enjoy it to its fullest, so I postponed it until that night. I read it as soon as I got home, no beer, no TV, no dinner (although I gave Ralph his), no walk, nothing until I finished. It was only 127 pages and plays are easy to read, of course, but I read slowly, trying to visualize everything. And then, when I got to the last page, about three o'clock, I think, I understood the final lines the way Tony must have understood them and felt them.

You'd have to read the play to know what I mean, but one of the main characters, Hannah, who has never found love, has a ninety-seven-year-old grandfather, Nonno, the "oldest living poet," who's been trying for many years to finish his last—and finest—poem before he dies. In the last scene, he finally completes it, brilliantly, hauntingly, dictates it to her, and gradually falls into a deep sleep. Hannah stays with him for a while, crying, then speaks to herself and the night sky:

"Oh, God, can't we stop now? Finally? Please let us. It's so quiet here, now."

3

SATURDAY AFTERNOON, MAY 10, was very warm, and Charley tended to stay in the indoor part of his cage, when he wasn't pacing. He was a five-hundred-pound, nine-foot-long Bengal tiger, eighteen years old, and the humidity made him very uncomfortable. Linda and I went to see him almost every weekend that spring. She would lean on the railing near the cage and talk to him in her quiet voice, and he always stopped pacing when she did that. He'd stand there, breathing faster than normal because of the heat, then he'd sit close to the bars and look at her. He was a beautiful animal. Linda had read his file in the public relations office in the administration building and found out that he was captured as a cub in India by the Trefflich Animal and Bird Company, and sold to the Central Park Zoo on November 14, 1962, for $1,500. He'd been confined to the same small indoor-outdoor cage ever since. It was in the long brick building called the Lion House, although there were only four lions in there, two to a cage. The other cages on Charley's side, all separated by steel walls, held a leopard, a cheetah, a black panther, and a big tigress named Princess. The entire opposite side held various families of baboons and gorillas. The Lion House had been built in 1934, and it was depressing if you loved animals as much as we did.

It was particularly depressing to Linda. She was finishing her sophomore year at NYU then and planned to study veterinary medicine after graduation, and she'd developed a real hangup about Charley. I don't think I realized how serious it was until that particular Saturday night. I took her to the QB III, a small restaurant-bar on Lexington near Sixty-seventh, owned by Bobby DellaRocca, the Giants' quarterback, and two partners. Then we were going over to Billy's Place, a jazz club where I had some business to check out.

The QB III was very popular that year and a lot of ballplayers and show-biz people hung out there. I remember the usual crowd of teenage girls out front that night. Some of them wore short-sleeved replicas of Bobby's football jersey with his name and number. They'd wait by the side of the canopy and maneuver to see who was arriving in the cabs. Then, if it turned out to be Nobody, the tone of their voices said it all.

I parked my cycle around the corner on Sixty-sixth, and Linda and I pushed our way through the kids. I nodded to Eddie, the goon at the door, and he let us in without the usual argument. It was one of our favorite places and we'd gone there at least a dozen times before he recognized us. He was a former heavyweight fighter and he looked like he had a fart caught in his brain. We walked past the crowded bar and Julie, the maître d', showed us to a table in the back room. There were huge action blowups of DellaRocca on the walls, but you couldn't see them very clearly in the candlelight. The jukebox was playing hard rock, and cigarette smoke hung in layers. The air conditioning didn't do much but circulate the smell of Italian cooking.

Most of the waiters knew us and didn't ask Linda for proof of age, but the one we got that night was new. When I ordered drinks, he tapped his pencil on the pad. He couldn't see much of Linda's face because she kept her sunglasses on.

"You got an ID I can live with, right?"

She took out her wallet and showed him her driver's license. I couldn't help smiling. She was going on twenty that summer and didn't look anywhere near it, and it pissed her off. When the waiter was gone, she pushed her glasses up on her head and glanced around. Her hair dominated everything, brunette, unusually thick, covering most of both profiles and down over her breasts. She was dressed a little more formally than usual, a new yellow blouse and her best jeans.

"Take a look at these assholes," she said.

"We'll have one drink, look around, that's it."

"Real classy clientele tonight. Pick up on that dipshit with the cigar in his face."

I glanced at the guy and laughed softly.

"That's you in ten years," she said.

I put my finger on the side of my nose, pushed it out of shape. "Maybe he's a *capo*, huh?"

"No. Lay you odds he's with the Parks Department. Central Park Zoo. Got to be. Angelo Dumppants, civil servant. Hired thirty-five years ago as a sweeper in the Lion House. Straight out of Sing Sing. They figured he'd feel right at home. Soon as they found out his brains were spaghetti, they gave him merit increases and promotions. Thirty-five years later, he's pulling down sixty grand, and his title is second assistant executive director, nutrition procurement, *Felis tigris*. Which means he orders horsemeat for the big cats. Takes a kickback on every pound."

I gave her a cigarette, lit it. "Don't forget he sells the catshit for fertilizer. Keeps his hand in right up to the elbow."

She smiled, blew smoke to the side. Her eyes looked great in the candlelight. "When I went up to the PR department? Ready for this? I go up there with my notebook and all, no shades, all smiles, Suzie Creamjeans, right? They got this blimpo sitting there, eating a hero sandwich. This is three o'clock in the afternoon, okay? This is no shit, he's sitting there, munching on a hero sandwich, reading the *Daily News*. Which he's dripping shit from the sandwich all over the newspaper. Okay, I stand in front of his tin desk. He doesn't look up. I clear my throat, I go, 'Excuse me.' He looks up at me with these heavy eyelids, still chewing away, he goes, '*Yeah?*' Like that. I go, 'Uh, excuse me, but could I please see the file on Charley, the tiger?' Blimpo chews a while, looks me up and down. Goes, 'File? *What* file?' No, I swear to God, this is straight, I'm not exaggerating. I go, 'I called up yesterday, spoke to the commissioner's secretary. I was told I could see the file, it's public record.' Blimpo goes back to reading his newspaper. 'Whaddaya want it for?' I go—I was all ready for this, okay?—so I go, 'Uh, like, I'm doing a term paper on him for my zoology class.' The son of a bitch keeps reading. He takes a huge bite out of his slob sandwich. I mean, you just wouldn't *believe* this guy. Then he goes—I could hardly hear him, his mouth was so full—he keeps reading and he goes, it sounded like, 'Um, Uma ma munchbake.' Daryll, I swear to God, I could've killed him when he said that. I felt like picking up something and slamming it into his skull. Then I thought: No. No shouting, no insults, nothing like that. I'd get him, I'd nail him, but I'd really make it *hurt*, and I'd make it *last*."

The waiter came over with our vodkas. Linda waited until he was gone. I held out my glass and we clinked and I took a long swallow. There was that first good burn that I always looked forward to.

"Do me a favor tonight," she said. "Do yourself a favor."

"Okay, okay."

"Just sip that shit, okay?"

"Come on, go ahead, what'd you do to Blimpo?"

She dragged on the cigarette. "After he hit me with that lunch-break thing, it was weird. I went from one extreme to the other. Like, I got very calm. I sat down. There was a chair on my side of the desk, and I sat down, leaned forward slightly, and stared at him. Didn't move a muscle, didn't say a word, just stared straight at him. Not a hard stare, not arrogant, not bitchy, just the opposite, okay? Soft and shy, kind of wide-eyed and blinking, with just a pleasant little smile. He glances at me, then down, then he does a double-take. I look away, bite my lower lip. He clears his throat, starts turning pages, right? I figured him to be about forty-five, somewhere in there. Pudgy face, bald pate, bushy sideburns. Maybe like five foot eight, but around two twenty. Flabby's the best word, a beer bloat. Polka-dot shirt, collar ends bent up, vomit tie pulled down. Fingers so fat he can't get the wedding ring off. I start looking at him again. Makes out like he's oblivious, but it's getting to him. Now, instead of sucking the mayo off his fingers, he's using the napkin. He's feeling it, knows what he must look like. Finally, he puts the sandwich down, scrapes back his chair, stands up, sucks in his gut as he walks around the desk, goes out in the hall. I'm alone in there. Grab my handbag, whip out my compact, check my face, brush my hair. This was a weekday, so I'm wearing my school stuff, workshirt, jeans, not that much bait, right? Okay, I'm braless, so I open another button at least. Cross my legs, show some good ankle, dangle—I was wearing my beat-up Scholl's—dangle one off my toes."

I had to laugh, visualizing it. As usual, she was acting out little bits, opening a button, crossing her legs.

She raised an eyebrow, pursed her lips. "Blimpo, he comes back from taking his leak, whatever. I'm reading my notebook now, swinging my ankle. Checks me out, clears his throat, goes around, sits down. All business: 'You want the file on—what was it?' Now I'm into my soft voice: 'No, *please* finish your lunch, I'm sorry I interrupted you, really, I didn't mean to.' That hits home. Blimpo's eyes change, posture changes, voice changes. Goes, 'No, no, that's perfectly all right, glad to help. You, uh, you're doing a term paper, huh?' I give him my little-girl smile. 'Yeah, right, on Charley, your tiger. He's beautiful.' Blimp goes, 'Well, you certainly picked a good one.' Gets up, sucks the gut, goes to one of the file cabinets. Place is lined with banged-up cabinets. Opens a drawer, pulls the file on Charley, goes, 'Yeah, I'm very fond of Charley. Happens to be one of my favorites.' I go, *'Yeah?'* He goes, 'Oh, yeah.' I go, 'Yeah, he's neat, right?' He hands me the file, checks my boobs, sits down. I go, like, 'Must be fun to work in such a big zoo, right?' He leans forward now, goes, 'Yeah, well, plenty of headaches, though. Lots of responsibility, you know?' I nod, smile, push back my long, lustrous hair, start reading the file. Then I let my sandal drop. Clunk."

She actually let a sandal drop under the table, clunk, and I laughed out loud. "You're a mean kid, you know that? Mean."

Again, the eyebrow. "I let it stay there, of course, I'm so interested in the file. Now Blimpo gets busy all of a sudden, wraps up his sandwich, folds up the newspaper, puts them in the desk, okay? Then he goes, 'Uh, look, there's a lot of material in there, honey, I can run off a copy of the stuff, if you'd like.' I go, 'Oh, wow, that'd be *neat*. But, like, I mean, I don't want you to go to any trouble, it's just a dumb term paper.' Blimpo's up in a flash. 'No trouble at all, come on, just down the hall.' Anyway, the bottom line. We're in the little Xerox room, he's running off the copies, asking me questions about my high school zoology class. Which, I never took a zoology class in high school, so I'm feeding him two tons of shit. But nicely, you know, like, 'When I graduate, I want to study veterinary medicine, that's my ambition.' Okay, he even collates the pages for me, puts them in an envelope. I thank him real sweet, then I kiss him on the cheek. Hard. Blimp, he's standing there, he doesn't know to shit or go blind. I go, 'Could I please come back tomorrow and like ask you questions about Charley?' He goes, 'Uh, I'd be delighted. Anything I can do to help.' Beads of sweat on his forehead now, okay? We turn to go. I hesitate, stop, look up at him. I go, 'You're really neat, I like you.' I kiss him on the mouth. Hard. Christ, I nearly threw up, okay? We walk down the hall. Not a word spoken. Lost in reveries of Lolita and Hum. Blimpo reaches in his back pocket, pulls out this smelly wallet that's like contoured to his fat ass, fumbles around for his business card. His hands are shaking. Gives me his card. Ready? Michael T. Shultz, Jr., *Director*, Public Relations."

"Director! Oh, no. No, come on."

She was laughing then. "No, I swear to God, I'll even show you the card. The thing is, he's a one-man office. You know, because of the city's austerity program? That's the whole department—*him.* So I went, 'Thank you, Mr. Shultz.' He puts his arm around my shoulder, he goes, 'Mickey. My friends call me Mickey.' I open my notebook, I write down my name and phone number. I figured, tell him the truth, get him to trust me, right?"

"Yeah, but why? What're you—"

"Because I got *plans* for that scumbag." Her voice changed then. So did her eyes and mouth. "Haven't worked out all the details yet, but I'm getting there. Every time I go into that Lion House I think about it. Every time I see Charley pacing around in that little shithole cage, I think about it. And I think about people like Mickey Shultz. The great minds that perpetuate torture like that. And invented torture like that. And are oblivious to torture like that. And I want to scream. And I want to cry. And I want to track down the people who did that and really hurt them. Not physically injure them. Just torture them so bad and so long that they'd beg to be free. Maybe you think that's crazy, but that's how I feel, okay? Every time I see Charley in there, I think: Christ, he's eighteen. He's been pacing around in there for seventeen years now and his normal lifespan is twenty. We wouldn't do that to a *dog*. We have too much compassion for that. I see Charley pacing in there, waiting, waiting, waiting for that one thing he's got to look forward to every day, that one pissy-ass meal at two-thirty. And I watch that zoo keeper squeeze out that chopped horsemeat from the plastic bag, that narrow plastic bag that's supposed to hold twelve pounds, but doesn't look like it does. And I watch Charley eating it like pablum, not even able to sink his teeth into it like he'd love to. And the worst thing of all, the thing that really gets to me, he's always careful to save half of it, right? Because he knows damn well that's it, that's all he gets for twenty-four hours. And he knows he's going to be hungry later on in the day, very hungry. So he's learned to save about half of it. He looks at that half on the floor, he licks at it, and his eyes say it all. He'd love to eat it all, but he knows better by now, okay? After seventeen years of being hungry. So he makes himself walk away. All right, it's too late for animals like Charley. But I'll tell you something. And, believe me, this is no shit. I'm going to make sure somebody bleeds inside their guts for that. I don't care how crazy that sounds. I don't care how adolescent it sounds, either. Can you . . . can you possibly dig that?"

"Yeah, I can. But you're chasing ghosts. You're screaming at ghosts. The mentality that built zoos like that, the people who built the Lion House, they're gone, Linda. They're dead. Figure it out, add it up. That was a different world. That house was finished in 1934, the date's right on the cornerstone, you've seen it. The people who came up with the idea, the people who designed it, they'd probably be in their seventies by now, if they're still alive. Figure it out, okay? Clowns like Mickey Shultz didn't have anything to do with it."

"Bullshit!" She stubbed out her cigarette, hard, then ground it to shreds in the ashtray. "He's a career civil servant. He's been employed by the Parks Department, in the Central Park Zoo, since he was twenty-one. He's just about what I figured him for, forty-seven, I saw his driver's license, okay? He's been in that department, in various jobs, for a full twenty-six years. He was an administrative assistant when Charley was sold to the zoo as a one-year-old cub."

"You really got the guy to open up."

"You kidding? Went back the next afternoon. Called first: 'Hi, Mr. Shultz, this is Linda Mercer. Could I please come in and see you this afternoon?' Slight pause, then his voice goes kind of deep: 'You certainly can, Linda, any time at all, you're always welcome.' I go, 'Like, I really need to see you, know what I mean?' Makes me puke to think about it."

She sipped her vodka and I waited for her to continue, but she didn't. I knew she'd tell me when she felt in the mood.

She was like that.

4

BILLY'S PLACE was then located on the corner of Second Avenue and Sixty-fourth Street, above Sal's restaurant, and the area was ideal for a jazz club, near a variety of movie theaters, restaurants, stores and specialty shops. The exterior of the three-story building was a clean red brick, recently sandblasted, and the windows were helped by attractive white louvered shutters. A large vertical sign hanging from the third-floor corner displayed Billy's logo on top, black lettering on a white drum with sticks, and Sal's logo below, both in bright spotlights. The club's entrance was to the right of the restaurant, topped by a small semicircular canopy, and there was a glass showcase next to the door, holding color shots of Billy in action and giving the times of the shows. Inside, a steep flight of carpeted stairs with mirrored walls led up to a coatroom, closed for the summer, and to the left were the heavy double doors of the club itself.

We arrived a little after ten o'clock (the first show on weeknights began at ten-fifteen), and the place was crowded, as usual, but I'd made a reservation. It was a relatively intimate room, cool and softly lighted by hundreds of circular white lamps hanging from dozens of thin, almost invisible poles, and you could see rows of red-and-white checkered tablecloths fanning out from the bandstand back to raised banquettes along the walls where photographs of Billy were individually lighted. A Sinatra album was playing softly as we were shown to our table in the back. I'd been there a number of times before, but it was Linda's first visit.

The music stands seemed almost luminous in that light, the same Slingerland custom jobs that Billy had used throughout most of his years with his big bands and replaced probably dozens of times: distinctive white marine pearl, matching the frame of his drums, with the familiar "BR" shield against two long vertical stripes. As the band came out, the houselights dimmed, the stage brightened, and—to Linda's surprise—the entire room went silent. Billy gave the verbal downbeat and they were into "Chameleon," a reasonably fast opener. Anthony Jack, the youngest of the group (I think he was about twenty), was on bass; Sonny Jones, alto and flute; Sal Garden, tenor; John Williamson, guitar; Jimmy Santos, conga; Kenny Rodney, piano. They looked smart in white suits and yellow turtlenecks, and Billy wore a white turtleneck and dark slacks. Each time one of them had a solo, he was hit with a spotlight, and when he finished, there was loud applause. It was a good audience. When the first number ended, they really exploded with applause, whistles and shouts. Then it was "Jumpin' at the Woodside," one of my favorites, written by Count Basie and John Hendricks, followed by the cool mood of "Cardin Blue," which Billy wrote himself.

There was a short break, during which Billy took the microphone, introduced the musicians, and told a few topical jokes in a low-key monologue—throwaway lines that were really very funny—and the crowd seemed to enjoy the poker-faced delivery almost as much as the punch lines. After the electrician set up two additional microphones, Billy introduced "a dynamic new singing group—three broads we picked up on the street this afternoon—the Dandelion Wine."

They received a good ovation as they made their way to the stage, wearing kind of funky denim outfits, and one of them was Chris Rees, Billy's tall, dark-haired, dark-eyed, twenty-year-old daughter. They sang several fast numbers and seemed to blend fairly well, and I remember it was difficult for me to take my eyes off Chris. Billy hadn't introduced them by name, so I didn't know who she was until later. She was anything but a polished performer, but she had a stage presence and a vivaciousness that was clearly lacking in the others, who were both her age, and she just seemed to be having one hell of a good time, snapping her fingers, smiling all-out, moving her body to the music, as if dancing in place. I don't know exactly what it was about her, but her whole attitude gave me a happy feeling, and I could see it reflected in Linda's face, too.

In honesty, I know very little about the finer points of show business. I see what most audiences see, the obvious. If I remember a particular performance for longer than a few days, it's an exception. But I recall that night vividly for a number of reasons, and one of them was certainly Chris Rees. At the risk of overstating the case, there was something magic about the girl when she was onstage, an electricity that you sensed more than saw or heard, an elusive combination of raw talents. What she would do with those gifts was not the question for me. For me, it was enough that I'd seen her trip. You can't really teach a singer to enjoy work *that* much, and I knew it couldn't be faked effectively at her age. It was unmistakable and it was exciting and it was also sad, in a way, because the vehicle for that kind of trip is delicate beyond belief.

After that, Billy and the band played for another half hour or so, and finished with a rock chart called "Giggles," in which Billy tangled delightfully with Anthony Jack on bass. They played around and against each other, carrying on a definite "conversation" with their instruments—soft, loud, sweet, sour, laughing, crying, loving, fighting—and, finally, it was time for Billy's solo. There had been bursts of laughter and staccato applause during "Giggles," but then, when the crowd somehow sensed it was time, the atmosphere in that room changed drastically. I remember the hush, and the way people leaned forward in their chairs, and the strong feeling of expectation: This is what they came to see.

I may be wrong, but it seems obvious to me that any solo by Billy Rees was so much more than the sum of its parts that any attempt to describe it was an exercise in music myopia. You had to experience the total phenomenon—technique, dexterity, speed, virtuosity, emotion—to catch even a glimpse of what it was all about. He was telling you something about himself in every solo, each one was different, and what he was saying just couldn't be translated into words. The man felt music so intensely that when you actually saw him, heard him, reacted to him, you knew instinctively that it was primitive emotion, not intellect. But more than that, you knew he was on a trip, whether he'd been smoking the stuff or not, and he usually had been. It was always a trip, a dimension of his own, where the distinctions between illusion and reality were not always clear to him. And where, I'm sure, it was often very lonely.

That night, when the solo ended, there was the split-second hesitation, and then it came, all at once, deafening. It came in the dark with only the spotlight on him as he made his way to the mike, dripping wet, using a towel to wipe his face, and it got louder. Louder when half the room stood up and shouted; louder when the houselights came on, changing the mood, illusion to reality, cigarette smoke drifting; louder than ever when he was up there, up at the mike, blinking, standing straight, listening to it, accustomed to it, feeling the vibrations, poker-faced, waiting, gauging the right moment, finally pointing with the towel to each musician as he introduced them again, but you could hardly hear the names. Anthony Jack was last, and there was a roar that lasted longer than the others, and then Billy motioned for us to sit, a slight wave of the towel, nothing extravagant, and it was over. It was like that when Billy played.

His dressing room was large and comfortable, on the top-floor corner, and that night you could see long lines of headlights, five lanes wide, moving south on Second Avenue, and hear horns and the steady hissing of tires on warm asphalt. Big color posters of Bruce Lee dominated the white walls, and the furniture was black, against a red carpet. There was a television set and a completely stocked bar. While Billy changed from his wet clothes, Linda and I talked with Nick Addison, his secretary. I think Nick was around twenty then, slim, well dressed, with thick black hair and a mustache.

He poured Linda a glass of white wine. "So, you a jazz fan, Linda, or what?"

"Absolutely."

"We like a lot of different stuff," I told him. "Right now we're checking out a British group called Tangerine Dream. Weird."

"I've heard them," he said. "Electronic synthesizers and sequencers, all that."

"Right," Linda told him. "They got synthesizers coming out their ears. Really unusual sound."

"Yeah, *sound,*" he said. "Daryll, you want a drink?"

"No, thanks, I'm fine."

Linda kicked off her sandals, sat cross-legged in a corner of the long black couch. Her hair looked terrific in the lamplight. She held it back with both hands while I lit her cigarette. I was very proud to have her up there with me.

Nick sat in the other corner of the couch. "Where you from, Linda?"

"West Tenth."

"Yeah? That's a beautiful area down there, tree-lined little streets and all, right? You go to school?"

"NYU, nights."

"What year you in?"

"Sophomore."

Billy came out in a bathrobe. He'd taken a shower, but of course his hairpiece was dry. Even in the robe he looked lean and hard and nowhere near his age. After I introduced Linda and all, he sat down, told Nick to lock the door, then took a joint out of his regular pack of cigarettes; he figured it was the safest place, which it was. He lit it, took a toke, inhaled deeply, held his breath, passed it to me. I did my trick of blowing out on it slightly, instead of sucking in. The tip lit up, of course, and I inhaled air, held my breath, passed it to Linda. She did the same thing before passing it to Nick. Linda and I just didn't dig pot highs, that's all. If you faked it well, like we did, nobody knew the difference and you didn't have to go through the whole thing of refusing and it didn't look like you were putting anybody down just because they happened to like it. We'd both smoked it from the age of twelve or something and we'd had bad trips on cheap stuff and it turned us off. Nick took a good pull before handing it back to Billy.

He flicked the ash, smiled at me. "Got the outline?"

"Does Basie have muttonchops?" I reached in my breast pocket, handed him the envelope. "Just five pages, but it'll give you the general idea."

He unfolded the manuscript, glanced at the first page. "Okay, up front now, Daryll. So I know where you're coming from. I'm not into writing, never have been. What makes you think you're qualified to do a job like this?"

I saw it coming and took a deep breath. I knew I couldn't con the guy much, so I looked right in his eyes and told it straight, with one exception. "The only biography, so-called biography, that's been done on you was that puffed-up, padded-out *New Yorker* profile, converted into a picture book—that's what it really was—published eleven years ago. Nineteen thousand words, tops. I've studied it carefully. It was a nice piece for *The New Yorker,* but I think it was a ripoff as a book. It doesn't even begin to tell your story. The guy who wrote it had a name in jazz circles—still has. I haven't. I'm nobody, I'm just entering journalism school next fall. But I know jazz and I know your work inside out and I know I could write a better book standing on my head. A full-length biography that you'd be proud of and proud to promote."

He nodded, handed the joint to Nick, started leafing through the pages. "What publisher you got in mind? What kind of bread we talking about?"

"Haven't talked to anybody yet. If you like the basic approach, the next step is a detailed outline of at least fifty pages, based on taped interviews. Then I'd make simultaneous submissions to half a dozen major houses, try to start a bidding situation."

Billy cleared his throat, put the manuscript back in the envelope and tossed it on the coffee table. "I'll read it carefully tomorrow, shoot it past my agent, see what he thinks. What kind of split you looking for?"

"Straight down the middle."

He nodded. "Nick tells me you work nights."

"I'm a janitor. Night person, like you. Get off work at

one o'clock. I could be up here every night at one-thirty, tape your life six nights a week every week. Six nights a week for—however long it takes."

"Six nights a week." He glanced at Linda, smiled. "What happens on the seventh night?"

She smirked. "It's your turn in the barrel."

Billy's eyes and mouth closed fast, his head went down, and he was into a soft nasal laugh, shoulders shaking. "Daryll! Christ, where'd you find her?"

"Met her when she was eleven."

"Oh, no. Not *that* routine!"

Linda leaned forward. "Wait a minute, wait a minute, it gets worse. My brother fixed us up. Believe it? Wait a minute, try this one: They were buddies in freakin' *Vietnam*. 'Daryll, wait'll you meet my sister! You think Jody *Foster*'s something? Wait'll you meet my *sister!*' Same number with me, right? And I'm eleven years old at the time. Thought he'd be a cross between Redford and Rockford. Took one look, thought I'd throw up. Looked like a shell-shocked four-eyed zero. Didn't date me till I was eighteen, thank God. Took me—first date, took me to a punk-rock joint down the Village. CBGB's, know it?"

"Yeah," Billy said. "Know *of* it."

"Thought I'd dig it because I was a kid. That kind of logic. Hated it. Absolutely loathed it. Then he starts talking sports, which means he's talking about himself. I'm listening. Finally, I've had it. I look at the guy, I go, 'Hey, tell me something. Strictly confidential. Who the hell you think you're jerking off here?' Got up and walked out."

Billy and Nick were laughing softly, enjoying her.

She gave her head the quick, familiar shake to toss her hair back. "Took a walk. Thought about him. Went back to the joint. It was quiet for a change, the band was taking a break. Found him at the bar. He's sitting there all alone and his eyes look like a stray puppy. Like, here's Daryll." She swung her legs down, turned her back to us, leaned on the arm of the couch, braced her chin on her fists. "So, I figured, this kid needs an upper, fast." She jumped up, walked to a stool in front of Billy's bar, sat down sideways, pretended I was on the next stool. "So I go, 'Hey, man, can I buy you an apple?' "

They were laughing, eating it up, and she even had me going. It was all true, and I wondered if she'd have the guts to go through the whole bit. I should've known better.

"He turns, he looks at me, he goes, 'What?' I go, 'Okay, an orange?' He's needing this, right? He hasn't got enough problems, here's this dizzy bitch sniffing around, probably flying on dust. So he goes—Christ, I could hardly believe it—he goes, 'No, thanks, I'm fine.' That number. Turns, gulps at his vodka, stares at it. You should've seen his eyes. Okay, decided to do an experiment on him."

"She's *always* experimenting on me," I said. "Never stops."

She gave me the eyebrow, then turned back to the invisible me on the stool. "I look at the guy—I'd had a few drinks, okay?—I look at the guy, I go, 'Man, it's hot in here.' Nothing. I go, 'Mind if I sit here?' Zero. Okay, it's hot in there and the air conditioning's not the greatest, so I unbutton my shirt all the way, tie the tails in front, up high." She did it with her yellow blouse, slowly, casually. "I was crazy with the heat, what can I tell you? Daryll, he's—from the corner of his eye, he's picking up on this, okay? Takes another gulp of vodka. I go, 'Wow, that's cooler.' I'm talking to myself. I signal the bartender. Comes over, takes in the cleavage and midriff, goes, 'All *right*.' I go, 'White wine, and another vodka for Mr.—what was it?—Travolta?' Daryll goes, 'No, thanks, I'm fine.' Now I look at the back of his neck, I touch it, reach under his shirt, searching. I go, 'Where's your pull-string, man? I think the record's stuck.' Then it happens. He laughs. Just a little tiny one, way down in his throat, but he can't help it, okay? I stick out my hand, I go, 'I'm Linda Mercer.' He shakes hands and smiles. The bartender goes for the drinks. Daryll goes back to his vodka. Doesn't even cop a glance at the equipment. Now I'm ready for the second half of the experiment. See, I'd read this news story about a ten-year research project by a woman psychology professor at the University of Illinois. She spent ten years conducting personality tests on guys of all ages and backgrounds to find out what kinds of men are attracted to which physical features of women. When it was all over, the results were very conclusive. Leg men tend to have much better personalities than—she called them breast men and buttocks men."

For some reason, that broke Billy up. It was the first time I'd seen him laugh all-out like that. He was bent over in his chair, laughing, clapping, stamping his feet, saying, "Knew it, knew it, *knew* it!"

Linda laughed softly. "This is straight, it was in all the papers. Breast men tend to be outgoing, flashy, independent, and unwilling to help other people. Ass men are orderly, socially dependent, self-abasing, and have guilt complexes. Leg men are socially active, willing to help others, and have more mature personalities. Okay, she didn't go into the *why* of it, she just stated the objective findings, right? So, where was I? Okay, now I knew Daryll wasn't a breast man. I'm relieved. Back to the experiment. I go, 'Man, it's really hot in here.' Zilch. Talking to myself. Ordinarily, I'm not into stuff like this, but the guy's eyes really intrigued me. Zip. Started to wiggle out of my jeans."

When she unzipped the fly, we were all laughing, but I don't honestly think any of us expected her to take them off. She took them off. Not turning away, not a hint of embarrassment. She was wearing her string-bikini bottom, the same light-blue one she'd had on in CBGB's that night. I remember there was a lamp on Billy's bar and she looked beautiful in the soft light. She didn't have a real tan yet, but her skin was naturally dark anyway, and she was slim, almost too slim.

Her voice didn't change an octave. "Wiggled them down, like so, which isn't that easy on a stool. Slipped off my sandals, pulled off the jeans. Rolled them up, like so, placed them on the bar, okay? Daryll's gulping vodka. I go, 'Wow, that's cooler.' Bartender comes over with our drinks. Checks out the roll of denim, checks the bikini, shrugs, goes, 'What do *I* know?' I slap down the bread, he takes it, rolls his eyes, splits. I turn to face Daryll, like so, cross my legs, hold out my glass. I watch the corner of his eye. It's squinting. I hear this soft, soft laughing sound. Bull's-eye. Daryll turns, he's breaking up. I watch his eyes. Flick—first to the bikini, then to the legs. I go,

'Cheers.' Clink. Gulp. Flick—eyes back to the legs. Up and down. I give him some ankle swing. Just enough, okay? Leg man. No question. Let him take me home that night. Even let him carry my denim roll. I figured, why break up a winning combination?"

5

I HAVE TO SMILE, looking back on that week. I was excited and anxious as hell to start the project as soon as possible, because I knew the fifty-page outline was critical and would take many weeks to put together—recording, transcribing, cutting, adding, rearranging and then rewriting. Since unsolicited material is generally ignored by major publishers, I already had a literary agent lined up. So, when the final draft was approved, all I'd need was a letter of intent from Billy giving me exclusive rights to do the book, together with his promise to promote it after publication, particularly on the network television talk shows like *Tonight*, where he was a frequent guest. But Billy played it so loose that first week, I was beginning to think he'd decided against the whole project. Nick told me to cool it, because Billy was moody and unpredictable. I was told to drop into the club any time I wanted, hang around, rap with him between sets and try to get to know him better. That turned out to be frustrating, because he never seemed to be alone. Never.

It seems crazy in retrospect, but I honestly believed I had a good shot at landing that project. I believed I could do it because I'd psyched myself into believing it. It was something of a shock when Billy turned me down at the end of the week, when he said he and his agent simply didn't think I had enough experience to do it. But it was a healthy shock, because it brought me back to reality. Like a lot of young people, I didn't like many of the realities of my life back then. The two years in Vietnam hadn't exactly helped, but I'd long since decided not to cop out on that, because it was too easy, it was too obvious. Those years hadn't helped, but they hadn't really hurt me that much. I was lucky. I wasn't really disabled. I'd damaged the lens in my left eye, not seriously, just enough to give me an astigmatism that required glasses to correct. No, I didn't like the realities I came home to, but I learned to cope with them because I knew I didn't have much choice. The fact is, Billy and his agent were absolutely right. I wasn't ready. I wasn't ready to do that book and I wouldn't be ready for years to come. Again, the whole idea was what my father would've called pie-in-the-sky bullshit, if he'd known about it.

When I told Aldo, he was disappointed, of course, particularly because I'd been so optimistic and positive about it. I mean, we even talked at some length about the advance Billy and I could expect from the publisher with the high bid. I was seriously thinking in terms of $50,000, split down the middle with Billy, of course, which would give Aldo and me just about half the amount we figured we'd need up front for the buy-out of the sporting goods store. That's the kind of heavy dreaming we were into. Well, you win some, you lose some.

One good thing, Aldo got through his first week on the new job without a hitch. He'd already joined the union, of course, Building Maintenance Employees Local 127, and paid his initiation fee; I'd arranged all that the previous Friday. We both came to work early his first night. I showed him around the building, introduced him to the two Polish guys on the day shift, took him downstairs, made sure he had a locker near mine, a complete set of keys for the various doors, and two sets of clean uniform shirts and trousers that fit. Well, one set of trousers was a little short, but still. After he was in uniform, we clowned around, I played a drill sergeant, shaped him up, inspected his gloves, shit like that. We were really feeling good, you know? Back together again. Genuine janitors! Hot *damn!*

That first week, I stuck right with him all the way, showed him the ropes, the whole routine, and he was beautiful. He loved it. Worked hard, too. I remember the first time we emptied the baskets from Mr. Long's office. He wanted to do it alone, he insisted, so I just stood back and watched. The guy broke me up. First, you have to understand the setup. Long and his son usually worked later than most of the other tenants; they were almost always there until six or six-thirty, okay? The thing is, they always put their trash baskets outside their door, which was just a little unusual. In the years I'd worked the job, I can only recall maybe half a dozen times I had to go in for them. So I explained all this to Aldo, and he goes, "Ah-hah!"

Okay, at five thirty-five, after finishing the lobby, we took the freight elevator to the second floor with our mop wagon, trash wagon and electric buffer. Like all the other floors, it had a long corridor with a stairway exit door at both ends, old marble walls, elevators in the middle, and a directory of tenants near the elevators. We swept the floor with pushbrooms, washed it with mops, rinsed it, buffed it. All the offices had company names on the frosted-glass windows of the doors, and all were dark and empty, save one. The last office at the front of the building near the exit was occupied, as usual, and the lighted glass door threw a pale-yellow rectangle across the clean floor. The sign read:

LONG & SON,
IMPORT-EXPORT

We started at the other end of the corridor, unlocked each office door, turned the lights on, grabbed the wastepaper baskets, emptied them in our trash wagon, returned the baskets, shut off the lights and made sure the doors were locked again. As always, when I slammed the door of the office next to Long's, his door opened, and his son placed two full wastepaper baskets on the floor, smiled at me, went back in and closed the door. He was a nice-looking Vietnamese kid, maybe twenty, twenty-one, and he usually wore his sport shirt out of his trousers.

The instant the door closed, Aldo went into action. He flattened himself against the wall, commando-style, eyes wide and wild, right hand tucked inside his shirt, glanced left and right, checked his watch, then did an exaggerated slow-motion tiptoe to the door, ducked under the lighted window fast. He emptied the baskets quickly with his left hand, placed them in front of the door, then—very slowly—removed his right hand from his shirt. Smiling like a madman, he pulled out a huge black rubber spider, held it gingerly with his heavy gloves, hung it on the edge of one of the baskets, then ran like hell down the hall.

Well, the first thing, I sprinted over and grabbed that freakin' spider like a shot, then tried to make it through the near exit door before I broke up, but I didn't quite make it. To this day, I don't know if they heard me or not. Behind the door, I just howled, I couldn't hold it in. That exit door was pretty thick, so it probably muffled most of it. I hope so. When I finally got myself together and went back for the trash wagon, Long's two baskets were gone, but he and his son were still working. I could see their silhouettes in the frosted glass.

Aldo had taken the freight elevator up to the next floor. When I got up there, he was curled up on the floor in front of the elevator, writhing in pain, holding the corners of his eyes back, playing Mr. Long: "Ahhh-eeee, Yankee poison meee! Phooey, phooey! I swallow all diamonds—he don't get sheeet!"

Yeah, and I was worried about Aldo getting uptight about the guy. Anyway, when we took our lunch break at eight-thirty that night, we went to McDonald's and tried to think of what to do with the big rubber spider. We wanted to keep it as a reminder of our first night together on the job. Down in our basement supply room, we had a bare light bulb hanging from the ceiling, and a long string was attached for a light switch. I always had trouble finding that string in the dark. So I attached the spider to the end of the string. Then we both sat back, had a cigarette and admired it. This is no shit, in that light down there it looked like a real black widow spider dangling at the end of its web. I mean, it was positively beautiful.

The following Saturday evening, Aldo and I went up to see the Yankee–Red Sox game at the Stadium. We had fairly good seats on the third-base side. Now, strictly speaking, we were National League men, but the-magic-is-back Mets happened to be in Cincinnati, and the Yanks were tearing up the league that spring. They won that night behind Tommy John (his sixth), with homers by

Nettles, Randolph and Jackson. Lynn had a solo blast for the Sox. We were celebrating Aldo's first week on the job, so we got a little pissed on beer. I know I had five, and I think he had six or seven. He also had four hot dogs. *Four*. With so much shit on them I couldn't believe it.

Sunday evening I went over to see Linda about seven. We were going to CBGB's later (she'd decided she liked it after all), which was within walking distance, so I left the cycle home and walked over to West Tenth. The West Village seemed to be changing faster than usual that year. I'd gone down there from Queens since I was about twelve, and watched it change, and in those years it had changed plenty. Like everything else, I suppose, but it gave me a bad feeling. Some of the changes were just temporary with the season and you could ignore them, but others had a feel of permanence. If you loved the place, as Linda and I did, and had good memories, the permanent changes were hard to accept. On summer nights, huge numbers of tourists always wandered around, picking up on what they thought were hookers and junkies and weirdos, but for the most part what they saw was just the usual packs of kids from Brooklyn, Queens and the Bronx, wandering around trying to look like hookers, junkies and weirdos. The real action had long since switched to the Minnesota Strip, a ten-block stretch of Eighth Avenue in midtown, but the majority of tourists either didn't know that or they'd taken one fast look at the Strip and decided, wisely, that it wasn't a safe place to even gawk. Anyway, they'd still flock to the West Village by the thousands on summer nights, then go back to their hotels, leaving the area somewhat worse than they found it, but not altered permanently.

The lasting changes were coming from another direction. That was the third year men had continued to drift over from the Bowery, to migrate over, really, in larger numbers every year, and I knew they were there to stay. In areas where the most permanent physical changes were obvious, they huddled in doorways with their wine or slept on the sidewalks back against the buildings, some in groups, and there were just far too many for the cops to handle on any given night. Of course, the usual small gangs of junkies were around that spring, too, nodding off on stoops and propped against buildings, and they were just as oblivious to the crowds and noise as the bums were, only much younger.

Way over on West Tenth, it was still a lot like it used to be. Linda was very lucky. She shared an apartment with a girlfriend on the third floor of a proud old five-story brownstone. The street was narrow and tree-lined, in the block between Hudson and Bleecker, and had long rows of brownstones that had once been townhouses. Most were apartments now, but with the high windows and ceilings, thick walls and working fireplaces that I loved. Almost all had big front stoops, too.

Linda was sitting on the stoop when I got there, wearing a navy-blue T-shirt, cutoffs, and rubber thongs. I wanted to get going to CBGB's, but I could usually tell when she just wanted to sit and be quiet and touch, so I shut up. It was quite warm. The dim streetlights made yellow patterns in the crowns of the trees and along the cracked slate sidewalk, and we could see other people sitting on stoops all down the block and hear their voices sometimes. Couples passed and an occasional car. A man walked past with a little Pekingese puppy on a leash. Linda knew the guy, said hi, ran down quickly, got down on her hands and knees and played with the puppy, saying its name, "Daisy," over and over. She looked great in the ragged cutoffs.

She came back smiling, sat on the step below me, stretched out, leaned back against the baluster. I remember her vividly, and the sound of her voice when she started playing her fantasy game. One of the things we had in common back then was our understanding and enjoyment of fantasies. Although I never told her my fantasy about Tony, that was mild compared to some of hers, particularly the one she started that night. The simple fact is, Linda had been overprotected by Aldo for so many years that she'd developed a habit of fantasizing resolutions to her frustrations rather than taking overt actions that might upset him or prove emotionally painful to her. It was a game I understood only too well. It was also a crutch, and a potentially dangerous crutch, because the longer you used it, the easier it became to substitute pleasant imaginings for hard realities. Over the past year or so, Linda had played progressively more complicated fantasy games with me, and I'd encouraged her. Still, she had an unusually fertile imagination, she played the game well, combining just the right elements of reality, and we had a hell of a lot of fun with it.

She glanced at me, arched an eyebrow. "Had a date with Blimp last night."

"Oh?" I knew she'd gone to see Reinhard Hauff's new film, *Knife in the Head,* with her roommate. "Want to tell me about it?"

"Heavy."

I waited a beat. Then: "How—? *How* heavy?"

"About two twenty, but he's on a diet."

"Want to tell me about it?"

"Naw."

"Not the intimate parts, I mean. Just the real gross stuff."

"Naw."

"Okay. Didn't want to hear about it anyway, to be honest."

Her voice went soft. "It was so . . . romantic is the only word. Met him in the Piano Bar on Bleecker. He said seven-thirty, so I got there at eight. He'd had two bottles of beer already, poor old dear, and he was sweating. An intimate booth, candlelight, piano music. 'Sorry I'm late, Mickey, had an argument with my mother. Told her I was going out with the girls, but she didn't believe me. So what else is new? She knows I dig older guys, she knows I date them.' Blimpo, he's very interested. 'How long you been dating older guys, Linda?' I'm biting my lower lip now, looking down, embarrassed. 'I don't know, about two years, I guess, since I was thirteen. It's just, guys around my age, even guys in their *twenties,* they're so—*awkward,* know what I mean?' He's nodding, the pig eyelids half-mast, he understands, he's been through it so many times. 'Perfectly natural. Perfectly natural, Linda.' Goes on like that. Waiter comes over, Chuck, remember him? Goes, 'White lightnin', Linda?' I go, 'Hi, Chuck, how you doing, man? Mickey, this is Chuck, he's cool, he never asks for ID.' They nod, smile, Chuck sticks out his hand, they shake—ha!—they shake *soul*-brother, right? Believe it? After that, after my first glass of wine, it's Gumdrop City time. Holding hands, staring at him. 'I really like you, Mickey, is that okay?' Ready for this? Blimp gives me a wink. This is no shit, here it comes, a slow, cool, conspiratorial *wink* from the rolls of lard. I'm telling you, I wasn't ready for that, I swear to God. I bite my lip, only this time it's not an act. I'm on the brink of breaking up, so I really dig my teeth in. For a second, just for a second, I thought I'd wet my knickers. Then it went away. Then, softly, 'Like, I need to see you more often, Mickey, know what I mean?' Lard-ass, he's sweating like a hippo in heat now. 'I want a picture of you, Mickey, is that okay?' He goes, 'I don't have no recent shots.' No, no, this is straight, that's exactly what he said. I'm into the little-girl-pout routine now. 'I want a picture for my wallet, so I can look at you any time I want.' He nods, he goes, 'I'll give you something else, I'll buy you a bracelet or something.' I go pouty-lips. 'No, I want a *picture* of you. For my—wait a sec. Chuck, I think Chuck has a Polaroid here. At least he used to. If he has, *please* let me take a picture of you? And you can watch it develop, and if you don't like it, you can tear it up, and I'll take another. Right? And I'll keep taking them and taking them till—oh, and it'll be *fun*, Mickey, okay?"

"Wait a minute," I said. *"Chuck's* Polaroid?"

She glanced up at me, pursed her lips.

"Chuck's Polaroid?"

"If you're a good boy and hold your water, you'll find out, okay? I lean across, I kiss him on the mouth—gently. *'Please* say yes?' I tickle his palm. His voice isn't too strong now, he goes, 'Oh, okay, let's ask him.' "

"I'm beginning to see the outlines of a—plan? Scam? Damn."

"Coming into focus? Stop staring at my legs."

"Your—? *Me?* I never, *never* stare at your legs."

"You—"

"Even if they *are,* uh, slim and brown and smooth and—well, kind of sexy. Me? I—I'd *never* do a thing like that. Never."

"You, uh, you want to touch them, kid?"

"Me? I—*I'd* never do a thing—"

"Just to see how . . . smooth they are?" She shifted her legs, braced her feet against the side of my left leg. "Go ahead. Have a—have a ball."

I remember I hung my tongue out and breathed like a dog as I stroked her legs. We were both laughing, then she slapped my hands away, pulled her legs in, hugged them.

Her little-girl voice: "That's all you get. For now."

"Decided I'm going to buy you a present."

"Yeah? When?"

"Tonight."

"When all the tourist stores are open."

"Lots of good stores, too."

"Whatcha gonna buy me? A bracelet, huh?"

"Nope."

"A *charm* bracelet to go with my personality?"

"Nope. An anklet."

She raised an eyebrow, then glanced at her ankles. "Always wanted a boy to buy me an anklet."

"Ever want a *girl* to buy you one?"

"Maybe. That turn you on?"

I smiled, looked away.

"Up *front,* Daryll."

"Yeah. It does. Okay?"

"Then say it."

She made me do that sometimes, say things out, when she sensed I had a hangup. Especially about sex-related things. It was hard at first, then I began to get used to it. I took a deep breath. "It turns me on to think of you wearing an anklet given to you by a girl."

"Would she have to be young? Pretty?"

"Oh, come on, Linda."

"Yes or no, then we'll drop it."

"I don't know. I guess so, yeah."

She thought about it, watched several cars pass. "What kind of anklet you going to give me?"

"A slave bracelet?"

"Knew it."

I laughed. "No. No, I had in mind a—handcuff. A single handcuff, with the chain hanging down. You know? Kind of jangling."

"So I'd think of you every step of the day."

"And I'd have the only key."

"So I'd have to be real nice if I wanted to get it off."

"No, actually, I had in mind a—strand of colored beads. Long enough to be wound around maybe twice. Colored Indian beads."

"That'd jangle as I walked?"

"Yeah, maybe. Would you wear that?"

She nodded, smiled, and I could tell she meant it.

"Done. We'll pick it out together, okay? Now back to Blimpo, come on. Sorry I interrupted."

"Okay, where was I?" She stretched out her legs again, crossed her ankles, folded her arms over her chest. "Oh, yeah. So I'd already set it up with Chuck, Friday night. Went over the details, he knew exactly what to do. Gave him my Polaroid One Step, flash attachment, loaded it, even had him take a sample shot. Saturday night, I call him over, ask if he's still got his Polaroid around. Yeah, sure, in his locker. Would he please let me take a shot of Mickey, we'd pay for the film? Sure, didn't know if he had any film in it, but he'd check. Chuck was dynamite. Comes back, goes, 'Wait a minute, got a better idea. How about if I took a shot of the *both* of youse?' Yeah, '*youse*,' you know Chuck. Anyway, before Blimp has a chance to blink, I laugh, lean across, pull him in for a cheek-to-cheek. '*Cheese!*' Flash, buzz, eject. Chuck pulls the print, goes, 'One more time.' I lean across, kiss Blimp on the mouth. Flash, buzz, eject."

"Splat, yuk, pee-you. Blimp dumps his pants."

"Shut up. We watch the prints develop in romantic candlelight. Takes about three to five minutes. Da-daaa, both come out sharp and clear. In fact, miracle of miracles, the cheek-to-cheek actually flatters Blimp-ass, okay? He holds it near the candle lamp, studies it, sweat dripping, eyelids heavy, like he might pop an orgasm any second. Goes, 'Not bad. You want it?' I take it away from him, gently, I go, '*Want* it? Of course I want it, ninny, I want both of 'em for my wallet. Man, you really look handsome in this one, look at your teeth and all.' We have more drinks, I want to know all about him, his whole freakin' life story. Blimpo's only too happy to tell me his whole freakin' life story. I'm hanging on every word, staring at him, mesmerized. Know what his wife's name is?"

"Don't tell me. Gertrude. No, no, Ursula."

"Florence."

I laughed quietly.

"Floor-ence. Calls her Flo. Got two kids, two daughters, one a high school senior in Bay Ridge, that's where they live, she's seventeen. The other, nineteen, a sophomore at CCNY. Now comes the heavy artillery. Flo and Mickey, they can't make it any more. Haven't gotten it on in—his words—'a long time,' okay?"

"Daughters turn him on?"

"He—wouldn't go into that. No. No, I tried a few very gentle—prods in that general direction. Like, 'Bet your daughters are real pretty, right?' Slurps his beer, nods, shrugs, looks away."

"Ooooh, yeah."

"Right? Old Flo probably lets 'em run around the house in frilly little—underthings? Living vicariously? Because of her tight-ass upbringing? Who knows? So, the way I figure it, Blimp probably locks himself in the bathroom frequently. Bay Ridge Fantasyland."

"Hope he sprays air freshener."

She swung her legs off the step, sat up. "Anyway, that's just about it for Phase One. Let's buy my anklet, then go to CBGB's."

"I don't get even a hint at Phase Two?"

"Not till you buy my anklet."

We walked east over to Bleecker, turned right and headed south, past Christopher, and the sidewalks started to get crowded down around Grove, Seventh, Jones and Cornelia, because of the open shops, bars and restaurants. The place where I'd already checked out some beaded stuff was called the Indian, a little shop on the corner of Bleecker and Leroy.

Linda knew the place and liked it. We went in and she looked at practically every anklet in the shop, tried on a lot of them, posed in front of the floor-length mirror, finally decided on almost exactly what I'd had in mind. I think it was actually intended as a necklace, although the salesgirl said it was definitely designed as an anklet, as I expected her to. It was a strand of red and blue beads that wound around twice, had a clasp, and fit just the way Linda wanted, kind of loose, so there was a slight clicking sound as she walked around the store. We both agreed it was perfect. I bought it and she wore it out, of course, and I thought it looked very sexy. She did, too.

We continued down Bleecker, past Carmine, and when we crossed Sixth Avenue (still can't get myself to call it

Avenue of the Americas) the crowds were really heavy. Bleecker heads southeast at that point and goes past the honkytonk tourist streets like MacDougal, Sullivan and Thompson, just below Washington Square. CBGB's was in the East Village at the very end of Bleecker, exactly nineteen blocks from Linda's house. But, in that direction, they were the "short" blocks, about a mile in all, and we always enjoyed that walk.

She told me about Phase Two on the way. "Blimperoo and I have a 'lunch' date next Wednesday. Uh, at my place? Noon to—whatever. I'll greet him—he'll be puffing and sweating from the walk up those stairs, so I thought I'd greet him in the nude. Well, wait a sec, don't want him to have a stroke and croak, do we? No. Maybe a string bikini might be better. 'See, Mick, I'm not allowed to run any of the air conditioners during the day, it's too expensive. We don't put them on till Mother gets home about six. So it's usually too hot to wear much around the house, y'know? Come on, I'll show you around, I'll show you *my* room first, it's really *neat.*' My bed will be unmade, of course, blinds and curtains drawn, just a soft glow from the little lamp on the bedside table. And, let's see, my stereo playing softly. No, no, what'm I saying? That's out. Has to be as quiet as possible for the tape recorder. Which, it'll already be running, naturally. My portable Sony with the built-in mike that can pick up on even a whisper from anywhere in the room. Know where it'll be? In the vent of my air conditioner, right smack next to my bed. With a brand-new one-hour tape."

I couldn't help laughing. "I think the legal term for that kind of thing is—uh—"

"Entrapment, right, when the cops do it. But here we have a little gem of a scam that's custom-tailored to bring down an indictment of the most devastating kind. Particularly when the tape's combined with Polaroid shots that everybody knows are almost impossible to doctor. Anyhow, soon as he steps inside, I close the door, smile, lock it, and we play kissy-face for a while, just to loosen him up a little. Maybe it won't be so bad in that kind of light. I'll do a lot of heavy breathing, but no verbal come-ons. Maneuver him over to the bed, snap off the lamp, slip off the bikini, tra-la-la, what can I tell you? Except I'll make him talk.

When I do my licky-ear bit, I whisper, like, 'I need the words, Mickey, is that okay? Don't know why, I just feel better when I hear the words.' He'll say everything I want, I guarantee it. After we get into the foreplay, I'll just talk to him in my normal tone of voice, get him used to the idea: 'When was the first time you knew you loved me?' Shit like that. 'Hey, you dig fantasies, Mick? Yeah, they're neat, right? I'll tell you one I have all the time about you, if you promise to tell one about me, okay?' I'll lead off with an S-and-M shot, like he ties me up and spanks me, and I love it, because I really need discipline from a father figure, that whole trip. 'Mick, I even have a couple of ropes in the drawer by the bed, because I thought it'd be fun to like act it out, y'know? Yeah, that'd be *fun,* right? What, Mick? Honey, please, I can't hear you, and I need the words, I really *need* them.' He'll talk. I'll torture him half to death till he answers every question, talks out at least a couple of trips, maybe acts one out."

"Scam," I said. "The revolutionary birth-control plan."

"Better than the pill, better than the diaphragm, better than rubbers, better than rhythm. Yes, you *talk* your way to satisfying, fulfilling orgasm, and avoid the old-fashioned, awkward and often embarrassing physical *yuk* of actual penetration. Not a cop-out, not a pull-out, Scam puts the *dignity* back in sex."

"How—? *How* much dignity?"

She arched the eyebrow. "How deep is the snow on a vampire's grave?"

6

THE NEXT TUESDAY NIGHT, MAY 20, Aldo had a serious run-in with Mr. Long. We'd been splitting up the chores that week, his second week on the job, working as a real team, which cut down the time spent on every floor by half, maybe less. Anyway, when we got to the second floor that night, I swept it, he washed it right behind me, I rinsed it, and, after it dried, we took turns on the electric buffer. Finally, we started going into the offices to empty the baskets, using two trash wagons; Aldo took the offices on the left side of the hall, I took the offices on the right. Okay, Mr. Long's office was the last on the left side, so I didn't see the whole thing, just the end of it when I heard the shouting and ran out to see. The way Aldo tells it, he slammed the door of the office next to Long's, waited for Long's son to open the door, as usual, and put the two wastepaper baskets down. Didn't happen on schedule. Aldo said he waited, looked in, saw two silhouettes through the frosted glass, so he knocked on the door. Didn't say how hard. Heard the old man's voice shout something, but it was too muffled to understand. Waited again. It was the last office on his side, of course, so he couldn't just move on. Knocked a second time. The old man shouts something again, inaudible. Couple of seconds later, the door swings open and old man Long himself slams the two baskets down, so hard that one of them tips over and spills trash over Aldo's shoes. Well, that's how he tells it, anyway.

Next thing, I heard two voices shouting and echoing in the hall. I ran out of an office just in time to see Aldo kicking the spilled trash at Mr. Long. I yelled at Aldo and sprinted toward him. Long's son was there in a flash and they were both screaming at Aldo in Vietnamese. Aldo was so goddam mad he was kicking the trash right into their office with both feet, calling them every name in the book. Wham, I grabbed Aldo around the waist, pivoted fast, flung him out in the hall, and Long slammed the door and double-locked it.

That was it. Over in a matter of seconds. Except Long and his son kept shouting at Aldo in Vietnamese from behind the door. Aldo just stood back, hands on hips, listening to them. He wasn't shouting any more, but he was so pissing mad his shoulders were shaking. I remember the expression in his eyes and the sweat dripping down his face. I didn't say anything or even go near him, but I kept an eye on him as I scooped up the trash, threw it in his wagon, then emptied the other basket. I gave his wagon a shove down the hall, went over to him, put my arm around his waist, and he walked away with me quietly. I had one office left to clean, but I just closed the door as we passed it and shoved my wagon down the hall toward the freight elevator.

We both took a break then. I checked my watch and it was just ten past six, so we took the elevator down to the basement, went in the locker room, had some instant coffee and a cigarette, and he explained exactly what had happened. He was still very, very angry. I did my best to calm him down, to let him know I understood, that I'd back him to the hilt if Long filed a complaint, and that seemed to help a little. The union allows ten minutes for coffee breaks and we were down there maybe fifteen minutes, but I figured it was worth it.

As I was rinsing the coffee cups, the phone rang, which was relatively unusual, but I half expected it. If not then, during lunch break. I dried my hands, answered it, recognized the voice immediately. It was George Fox, maintenance supervisor of the real estate firm that owned the Waring Building. George was a bright, good-natured guy, he'd always treated me fairly, and I liked him a lot. If you had a problem, you could always talk with him. He'd listen. He'd try to help.

"Daryll, I'm home, I just got a call from one of the

tenants. Long, Mr. Long up in two twenty-one. What the hell happened up there?"

"Nothing, no big deal. One of his baskets spilled."

"Daryll, look, listen to me, okay? Now, Long, Mr. Long, he's going crazy up there. I'm telling you. What's—what is he, Chinese?"

"Vietnamese."

"Yeah? You wouldn't believe this guy. Practically screaming at me. I mean, he was so freakin' mad he could hardly talk. Finally, his son gets on the line. Introduces himself, very polite and all, he says the new man insulted his father. Says he kicked trash at his father, kicked trash at him, kicked it right into their office."

"Okay, wait a minute."

"Says, 'The new man, the new man.' Then his father gets on the phone again, says he wants the new man *fired*."

"Oh, George, for Christ's sake. Mr. Long spilled the basket *himself*. Aldo says the old guy slammed it—"

"Is Aldo there now?"

"—down so hard it spilled all over his shoes."

"Let me speak to Aldo, huh?"

"That's what happened, George, he'll tell you the same thing."

"Look, listen to me, okay? I got to speak to Aldo. I know what you're trying to do, I understand, but the kid, the son, he says you weren't even there till it was almost over. That right?"

I took a deep breath. "Yeah. But I saw what—"

"Please, let me speak to Aldo."

"Right." I waved Aldo over, clapped my palm over the mouthpiece of the phone. "George Fox. For God's sake, stay calm. Just tell him the truth."

He nodded, took the receiver. Actually, he stayed quite calm through most of the conversation. He explained what had happened, almost exactly the way he'd told it to me. Then he admitted he was wrong to kick the trash at them. From that point on, I don't know what George was telling him, but he started to frown, tried to interrupt a couple of times, then really got hot and began giving George an argument, you know, really spitting the words out. I tried to grab the phone from him, but he shoved me away. Then I could hear George's voice yelling back at him, taking charge, talking him down. Aldo shut up for a while and listened, sweat dripping from his face. His last words to George were: "I'll be there! You bet your ass I'll be there!" He hung up so hard the bell in the phone rang sharply.

We looked at each other in silence.

Aldo shrugged. "I think I've had it."

"What?"

"Slant-eyed alien scumbag."

"He can't have you fired. We got a union."

"Yeah, well, George says to be in his office nine o'clock tomorrow morning. He'll have the union rep there. Long claims I kicked him in the legs, twice."

"That's a lie!"

He gave me a look.

"Oh, shit."

"Daryll, listen, I don't know, okay? It's possible. Everything happened so fast, I don't know. I went like crazy, okay? Anyhow, Long claims I kicked him in the legs, twice. Told George if I don't get fired he'll swear out a warrant for my arrest. Assault and battery, and he's got his son to back him up. And he says he's got the bruises to prove it. What can I tell you? I'm suspended until the meeting."

"I'll go with you. I'll be there to back you up."

He shook his head. "George told me specifically he didn't want you there. Says you didn't even see it till the end, you admitted it, and he doesn't want to complicate the thing by hearsay. Says Long and his son will be there with their attorney. Said I could have an attorney present if I wanted. Said I'd have a very fair hearing."

"The union guy will definitely be there?"

"Yeah. Guy by the name of Bill Johnson."

"You want an attorney?"

He thought about it, frowning, then nodded, pursed his lips, narrowed his eyes. "Uh, yeah. Yeah, I do. I want F. Lee Bailey."

I played it straight. "Good choice."

"Yeah. Yeah, F. Lee Bailey from South Ozone Park, Queens, good buddy of mine. Specializes in defending janitors against shin-kick assault claims by elderly South Vietnamese diamond hustlers. Top man in his field. Real name is Fang Lee Baywee, a former Cong general. I figure, if anybody can get me out of this, it's a Cong. I mean, shit, they won the war, didn't they?"

The hearing was held at nine sharp next morning in George Fox's office. Aldo was there on time, wearing his best suit; the union guy, Bill Johnson, was there, apparently angry as hell; plus Mr. Long, his son, and their attorney. Now, I only know what Aldo told me, but after a lot of bickering back and forth, it boiled down to this: Mr. Long's attorney stated that his client would definitely swear out a warrant for assault and battery unless Aldo was discharged from his job immediately. However, if he was discharged forthwith and prohibited from entering the building, Long would drop the assault-and-battery shit. Bill Johnson to the rescue with a compromise: Aldo would be allowed to keep his job, but: (a) he'd be suspended for a period of thirty days without pay; (b) he'd be permanently barred from working the second floor; (c) he'd be forbidden to have any future contact with Mr. Long and his son; (d) he'd apologize to Mr. Long and his son in writing.

Okay, according to Aldo, Mr. Long's attorney responded to the compromise suggestion by opening his attaché case, withdrawing copies of a legal document and passing a copy to everyone present. It was Mr. Long's office lease. The following sentence was underlined in red on each copy: "And the said Lessor covenants with the said Lessee that he has good right to lease said premises in manner aforesaid, and that he will suffer and permit said Lessee (he keeping all the covenants on his part, as hereinafter contained) to occupy, possess and enjoy said premises during the term aforesaid, without hindrance or molestation from him or any person claiming by, from or under him."

After letting that sink in, the attorney then calmly explained that the lease had obviously been violated, that Mr. Long had been insulted and assaulted on the premises by a salaried employee of the lessor without provocation, and that if the employee was not dismissed, effective immediately, Mr. Long would initiate legal proceedings against the lessor for "a very substantial amount of money."

At that point, George Fox and Bill Johnson asked to be excused for a private conference. They went into the next room and left Aldo sitting there with Long & Son, neither of whom would even look at him, and the distinguished attorney, who chose to inspect his manicured fingernails.

The private conference lasted about five minutes, tops, and the two men returned silently. George Fox sat down, cleared his throat, and spoke to the attorney in a cold monotone: "Under the circumstances, we've decided to terminate Mr. Mercer's employment, effective immediately."

For some reason I still can't quite understand, Aldo believed Mr. Long would cool down in time, reconsider, and eventually accept an apology, if it was offered in the right way. He said the way he understood the Oriental philosophy, the fact that Long had been kicked wasn't the primary issue at all, it was the insult that mattered. Mr. Long had been insulted in front of his son. Therefore, recompense must be exacted, or Mr. Long would lose face. However, if Long reflected on the issue and realized that maybe the retribution had been too severe for the degree of insult, he might be persuaded to accept a sincere apology, in the presence of his son, of course. I didn't agree with him, and I told him that, straight out, but I said I'd try to help in any way I could.

His strategy was to approach the whole thing in gradual stages. First, on Friday evening, he wanted me to have a word with Mr. Long to sort of break the ice for him. Just a short, friendly little chat, in which I'd mention that I was personally very sorry about what had happened and all, particularly because Aldo had been my best friend for so many years. I'd say that I felt personally responsible, because I'd gotten him the job, so I felt awful about it and hoped he'd forgive me. Then I was supposed to play it by ear. If there was the slightest attempt by Long to continue the conversation, I could go on to say how we were buddies in Vietnam, that Aldo had had an extremely rough period of adjustment, blah, blah, blah, whatever I thought, up to the point when I'd say how broken up Aldo was about the whole mess, and how ashamed he felt about it. No more. Well, I didn't particularly like that approach, but I thought it was worth a shot.

Friday evening, May 23, was the start of the big Memorial Day weekend, and a large percentage of the offices in the building closed a little early in an attempt to beat the mad rush out of town. In all honesty, I was half hoping Mr. Long and his son would leave early, too, because I didn't really feel like approaching them that night; I felt it was too soon.

Anyway, after I finished the lobby and took my stuff up to the second floor, I glanced down the hall quickly, hoping their lights would be out. They were on. It was about six o'clock, or close to it, and that was the one and only lighted office on the floor. Well, I figured they could always leave while I was sweeping or washing or buffing, and I wouldn't have to go through the whole embarrassing thing of knocking on their door, you know, I could have a quick chat in the hall, or maybe I'd really luck out and be in one of the offices getting baskets when they passed. So I took my time that night. Really stretched it out.

At six thirty-five, they were still there, and I was emptying baskets in the last few offices, so I resigned myself to it. I slammed the office door next to theirs, wheeled the trash wagon along, heard their door open and close faster than usual. The two full baskets were on the floor; I'd missed seeing the son by a few seconds. One thing about the kid, he read a lot of magazines in the office, and I used to look at their baskets more carefully than the others. That night there was a recent copy of *Time* in one of them. I put it in my back pocket, emptied the baskets, then plopped them down harder than normal so the son would be sure to hear. Next, I gave my trash wagon a shove down the hall; its wheels squeaked. I remained next to the door. I could see their silhouettes through the frosted glass. One of them walked toward me.

The door opened and the son smiled quickly and nodded as he leaned over for the baskets.

I smiled, too. "Could I have a word with Mr. Long?"

He turned, asked his father in fast Vietnamese. The old man was studying a diamond through an eyepiece. He didn't even glance up, just replied in a couple of quick words. The son turned back to me, hesitated, as if trying to think of a polite translation.

"It won't take a minute," I told him. "It's kind of important."

The kid nodded, relayed the message, but Mr. Long interrupted him, sounding annoyed, and came to the door. He was a short, slim, wiry man, gray hair receding, but his age would have been difficult to determine if you didn't get a good look at his eyes. They were cold, clinical, appraising, the eyes of a man who gave no quarter and expected none.

His tone was sharp. "So? Yes?"

"It's about Aldo, Mr. Long. Allan Mercer. You see, maybe—I think you just misunderstood."

He lifted his hand slightly, shook his head. "He was not very nice. He made an insult, and that—I do not tolerate." His smile really surprised me; it seemed genuine and friendly. "Have a nice Memorial Day. Don't work too hard."

He ushered his son inside and closed the door, not loudly, but with finality. Well, nobody likes to have a door shut in his face, but at least it wasn't done rudely. I remember standing there for a few seconds, thinking of all the things I should've said, the stuff Aldo told me to say. For just an instant, I considered trying again. Then I thought: Screw it.

I took my lunch break about the usual time, eight-thirty, then decided to get some paper baled. In the basement, we have this enormous solid-steel paper baler, like a truck-sized trash compactor. It stands maybe fifteen feet high and six feet wide. You empty trash into the top of the machine from the edge of a landing. When it's full, you press a button at the base and the lid moves down slowly to compress the trash with tremendous pressure per square inch, compacting it from a height of fifteen feet down to about five feet. Next, you open the front door of the machine, attach loose baling wires, and press another button. The lid pulls up, the paper expands, the wires tighten, the bale is ready. You yank it out onto a dolly, wheel it away, then start all over again. Only trouble is, the machine needs a grease job badly and the mechanic hasn't gotten around to it. During compression, it makes a sound like God almighty tearing the tin roof off a barn with his bare hands. Like anything else, you get accustomed to a sound like that, but it takes a while. First time I heard it, forget it. Scared the piss out of me. Literally. Not all that much, but still.

Something strange happened that night. I remember I'd compacted about four bales, and I was sitting there reading a copy of *The New Yorker* that I'd found in somebody's basket. As the last bale was being pressed, right in the middle of all that noise, I thought I heard something move over near the furnace. Ever have that happen—you're oblivious to a constant noise of some kind, your ears are desensitized to it, but you pick up on another sound? I glanced around carefully, didn't see anything unusual around the furnace, but of course the lighting down there is always dim at best. When the compression cycle was completed, the machine shut off automatically. In the abrupt silence, I sat there and glanced around again, listening, concentrating. Didn't hear the sound again, but I just sensed the presence of something or somebody over near the furnace. Gave me a very bad feeling. The only means of protection I had was a steel pipe, a foot-long steel pipe that I kept on a ledge near the baler. I glanced up to make sure it was there, then concentrated on the area around the furnace again.

In the dim light, I thought I saw the tips of a man's shoes. I stood up cautiously, walked slowly to the ledge and grabbed the pipe. Took another look from that angle. They were definitely the tips of somebody's shoes, standing sideways behind the bulk of the furnace. I considered running, but to get out of that area I'd have to pass relatively close to the furnace, then turn my back before I took off. So I figured I didn't have much choice but to face the guy. That way, at least I'd have some control. I gripped the pipe hard, took a deep breath, moved very slowly toward the furnace. I was wearing sneakers, so I knew he couldn't pick up on my steps that much. As I got closer, I could see my shadow distorted by the contours of the furnace. When I felt I was close enough, I stopped, got set, then made a sudden move, a quick feint to the left. The tips of those shoes didn't move a fraction. They were black, well shined, expensive-looking. I waited a few seconds, stepped close against the furnace, swung one foot out, kicked at the shoes, jumped back fast. The shoes were empty.

The instant I realized that, I saw the shadow of a man on the wall directly ahead. He was standing behind me. I'd bought it. Just a rinky-dink, jive-ass variation on the theme of deception that you pick up in the service. Part of learning to be a professional killer. After eight years, my instincts weren't that sharp any more.

I spoke softly. "You're right behind me, Aldo."

Silence. I turned. It was him, smiling. Maybe it was the dim light down there, but he looked a little dumpy. His shirt, tie, sport jacket, even his belled slacks, all looked like he'd slept in them. Knowing him, he probably had. He kept smiling, walked past me, stepped into his shoes.

"You're not supposed to be here," I told him.

"Nobody saw me. Bad day today?"

"You know what it's like on Fridays."

"Yeah."

When I went back and put the steel pipe on the ledge, my hand was still shaking. I knew he was dying to hear about my talk with Long, and I didn't know how to tell him. I suppose I felt guilty about the way I'd handled it. I watched as he went to the old bookcase we had down there, picked up a copy of *Playboy* and leafed through it. There was a long pause. I felt for the guy in those moments. I really did.

He tossed the magazine aside. "You talk to Long?"

"I tried. His mind's made up. He says you insulted him."

He tried to keep his temper. *"I* insulted *him?* Is that all he said, *I* insulted *him?"*

"Hey, come on, you know how he—"

"He flung the goddam trash cans at my feet. Just threw them down. The stuff spilled on the floor."

"You know that was an accident as well as I do."

"Sure, maybe it was an accident that I kicked that shit back into his office. Slant-eyed mother."

I walked over to the baler, and he followed me. I unlocked the heavy steel door, pulled it back all the way, attached the loose baling wires, then pressed the button.

The lid moved up noisily. I watched the paper begin to expand and the wires tighten around it.

Aldo had to raise his voice a little. "It's some country we're living in. Getting fired over a gook like that."

"He's a tenant, Aldo."

"Isn't that the shit? I'm asking you. Isn't that the goddam shit? For two years in Vietnam we clean up and mop up for them. Then we come back to *our* goddam country and they're *here*. They're all doing *fine*. Man, there's Vietnamese all over the place, got their own business, doing fine. And we're cleaning up and mopping up after them all over again. I'm asking you, isn't that the goddam shit?"

"You know what? It is. You know what else? That's just the way it is."

"What the hell did I shoot the Cong for?" He hesitated then, glanced at me, had to look away. "The Cong were all right. They stayed in their own country. It's the bastards from the South. You see the papers the other day? The old mayor of Saigon, he's running a *pizza* place. Huh? I'm asking you."

The bale was ready. I pulled it out of the machine, wrestled it onto the dolly. "Listen. If you want, I'll talk to Long again next week. Maybe by then he'll—"

"Nah, the hell with it. If I can't bring myself to apologize without any preliminary bullshit, I'm not worth much. I'll speak to him myself next week. He'll have the whole three-day weekend to cool down." He smiled then, slapped me on the butt as he started to leave. "Hey, do yourself a favor, huh?"

"What's that?"

"Watch out for that guy behind the furnace."

7

THAT SATURDAY NIGHT, Linda and I went to CBGB's. It was the first punk-rock bar in the city, 315 Bowery, between First and Second streets. The owners had opened an uptown branch, a much classier spot, but Linda and I liked the original one. First, because we'd had our first date there, the wild one, but also because it just seemed more earthy and spontaneous. You could drop in there wearing just about anything you wanted, from a bikini on up, literally, and it was done, and nobody hassled you. The area was so bad-ass and dingy that the bar's little white semicircular canopy stood out in contrast, with its cheerful red letters, CBGB, and on the little fringe under that, UMFUG, the name of its recording company. The only thing was, it was a rummy neighborhood, with men sleeping in doorways and shit like that, so the place had to have black steel gates across the front. They were rarely opened all the way, because they protected the big front windows, so you never got the full effect of the white stucco facade.

Outside, you could hear the buzz-and-blast music all over the block. There was an old hotel right next door, the Palace Hotel, and that's the only thing I felt sorry about. I felt sad about the men in there trying to sleep. What can I tell you? I think about stuff like that. Sometimes I imagine myself in one of those rooms, trying to sleep one off, and not being able to do a damn thing about the noise. Then I think: Oh, hell, if I had a muscatel high like those guys, I'd sleep right through the noise anyway. And I would, too.

Anyway, we got there about eight-thirty. There was a

hand-painted sign on the door, *Audition Showcase,* which meant that a variety of new groups would be playing, so we knew it'd be interesting. The place was packed, as usual. I paid the four-fifty cover for two, and we got our hands stamped in red ink so we could come and go. The month and day were right, May 24, but they always dated it one year ahead. There was a long, old-fashioned bar to the right with a bunch of small neon beer signs jutting out overhead, an area of jammed-in tables with candle lamps to the left, the big sound-system control console in front of that, then another section of tables extending all the way up to the low stage. No dance floor. Rock posters were plastered all over the walls and even the stage, and the ceiling was just a series of bare pipes. We really liked the place. It wasn't the jam or the music or the smell of pot, it was just that we felt very comfortable in there.

I remember that night especially well, because Linda told me about her fantasy lunch date with Mickey that week. No preliminaries, nothing, she just launched into it, every detail down cold, as if it had actually happened. It was during one of the long breaks, and we were sitting at a little table in the corner, to the left as you came in, near that big front window. I can see her clearly now. She'd washed her hair that afternoon and it had body and a dark sheen, and her eyes seemed transparent in the light from the candle lamp. Her voice had excitement in it, and conviction. That was the spooky thing about the Charley fantasy, as opposed to the others. She was so deeply into it, I'd catch myself wondering if she really *did* believe it. Or, worse, if she'd actually *done* all this shit with Mickey. I mean, if you were sitting at the next table that night, eavesdropping, you wouldn't have a clue. You'd believe every word.

She told me she'd executed the whole date just about the way she'd planned, and the poor son of a bitch had bought it. She'd made him sweat it, and she'd made him talk plenty. She couldn't get him to act out any of the S-and-M fantasies, he was just too inhibited, but she'd finally tormented him into telling her two of his. They were predictable enough, relatively tame, and sad in a way, and she said his voice shook badly through both. I'll spare you the details, except to say when I heard them, and the way her voice shook when she imitated him, I couldn't help glancing sideways to see if the couples at the nearby tables were listening. They weren't, thank God.

I suppose all outstanding actors and actresses have to get into fantasies as deeply as Linda did, or even deeper. I guess they have to have such vivid imaginations that they actually cross some invisible line in the mind between illusion and reality. But I have to admit the idea has always been a little unnerving to me when carried to the extreme. Reason? Knowing myself, I suspect that I might very well carry it to the extreme. Granted, we all play fantasy games, passively, when we watch a television drama or a movie or a play or read a compelling novel. All of us. We make a conscious decision to suspend disbelief, temporarily. As soon as we turn on the set or enter a darkened theater or open a book, we freely, gladly, even anxiously, choose fantasy over reality. And most of us do it consistently. For the obvious reason that most of us can tolerate just so many hours of reality in an average day. But then, when the film or play or novel is completed, the majority of us can snap out of it and make the mental adjustment back to reality again, no matter how painful or frustrating or boring it might be. That mental adjustment is precisely what unnerves me. Because, more often than not, I don't want to return to the reality of my life. I want to go on dreaming. I want to invent reality. And, seeing Linda's eyes that night, hearing her excitement and confidence, I envied her deeply. I knew where she was coming from and I wanted to be there, too. You don't need drugs to enter that dimension, you don't even need alcohol. All you need is the imagining mind. And, God knows, Linda had it.

She snapped out of it periodically that night, long enough to embellish the thing with reality. I remember the way she blew smoke toward the candle lamp, narrowed her eyes as she watched it curl upward. "When Aldo and I went out to the San Diego Zoo two years ago? Two summers ago? Never realized how much of an impact it'd have on me later. The world's largest collection of wild animals. Over five thousand specimens of fourteen hundred species, okay? Living in natural surroundings, modern, humane, cageless confinement. Then, the next day, when we went to the Wild Animal Park, I couldn't believe it. I'd never seen—I'd never even *heard* of anything that beautiful. I mean, what'd *I* know? Here's this eighteen-hundred-acre preserve, enormous, where more than a thousand animals roam around in herds. As close to free as I'd ever seen. In an environment that closely resembles their native habitats. I think I told you, we went through on this electric monorail? Called the Wgasa Bush Line. Part I liked best was the East Africa section, reserved for rhino, elephant, lion, tiger, giraffe, antelope, like that, the big animals. Anyway, I've never forgotten. Never will. You come back, you compare that with old-fashioned, conventional zoos like ours, you realize—for the first time—what cruel anachronisms they are. They should be legally abolished. Someday they will be, all of them. But it's a political problem, as usual. It's a complicated political problem that's been fought for years by the ASPCA and other organizations. And nothing's happened. Nothing's changed. Take the Lion House, right? Nothing's changed in there, nothing of any significance, in *forty-six years*. That's why I've decided to stage a very personal . . . 'demonstration,' we'll call it. A demonstration against conventional zoos in general and the Central Park Zoo in particular." She looked at me, smiled. "And it's going to be a breeze, thanks to Blimpo. We're going to steal Charley from his cage. And Lard-ass is going to help us."

"Steal?" I said softly. "Charley?"

"From his cage, yeah. Phase Three is coming up. In a way, it'll be the easiest of all, because the foundation is solid. We have leverage. We have power. We have Mickey Shultz's balls in a steel vise. He doesn't know it yet, but he will. Next week. When I start squeezing. I start Tuesday morning, bright and early. Call him at the office, okay? 'Hi, Mickey, it's me, how you doing? Great. We should have more lunch dates, right? Listen, honey, I was thinking about you this morning and I wanted to share something with you, is that okay? Okay, just wanted you to hear part of this really neat album I bought. Wanted to share it with you. It's a new sound and the lyrics are dynamite. I know you're busy, but could you just listen for a minute? Great. Okay, here goes.' "

I felt something like a cold shiver. "Jesus Christ."

Her eyes, mouth and voice changed as she leaned forward and nodded. "Right? I'll let him hear a full minute of the most damaging part I can find. Then I'll cut the little-girl crap and stick it to him. There'll be a deadly silence on his end. Probably hear him breathing. 'Okay, scumbag, now listen and listen *hard*. Know what that is? That's *statutory rape*. Open and shut. I plan to do two things, immediately, unless you cooperate and do exactly what I tell you to do. One, I plan to deliver a copy of the tape and Xerox color copies of both Polaroid shots to the police, claim rape, and swear out a warrant for your arrest. Two, I plan to deliver a copy of the tape and copies of both Polaroid shots to the Parks Commissioner and inform him that I'm pressing charges."

I nodded. "He's got no choice."

"You better believe it."

"Let's hear the whole shot."

"We can't wait long, so I figure next Friday. Early evening. You'll have to take that night off, and that's all I'm asking. Call in sick. Don't know what kind of security they have, probably a night watchman, but Blimp will handle that. And he's got access to all the keys, so that's no problem. Closing time's five o'clock. Most of the office staff splits out of there on the dot. The vets, too. I'll meet the Blimp in his office at five, explain exactly what's expected of him. Five-thirty, we go to one of the vets' offices, pick up the tranquilizer they use on the bigger animals. Next, the kitchen, pick up a ration of horsemeat, saturate it with the tranquilizer. They use—ready for this? For the tranquilizer, they use a mixture that includes PCP."

"Dust? No."

"Yeah! *Dust!* Used it for *years* on the big animals, whenever they had to examine them or move them, okay? Like, Charley had two minor operations when he was younger, it's in his file. He was flying on dust before anybody ever *heard* of it. Probably *loves* the stuff, wonders why they won't give him more. Anyway, next, over to the Lion House, lock the door, feed him the horsemeat. That'd be about six, six-fifteen, somewhere in there. Takes at least an hour for the tranquilizer to take effect, I've checked that. He's drowsy in an hour, asleep within two hours. Depends on how much he moves around first. Could be faster if he does a lot of pacing after he eats. We'll plan on eight o'clock. In the meantime, the maintenance crews start at six every night. From what I could find out from Blimp, they hose down the cage floors and stuff between six and seven. He wasn't sure, of course, because he's never seen such peon work. Anyway, if any maintenance people come in while we're feeding him, so what? I mean, hey, we're talking about the *Director* of Public Relations here, Michael T. Shultz, *Junior*, no less, what're you, kidding? 'Uh, hello there, Maintenance. A-hum, uh, just showing the little lady how it's done, ha-ha. For her school term paper, you know, ha-ha. Don't hose out the, uh, excrement till we leave, okay?' Next, we wait in Blimp's office until seven forty-five. That's when *you* come into the picture."

"Knew I'd make it."

"Next Friday, you have to rent two things—an electric forklift truck with a pallet, and a good-sized van, an RV, okay? Get one with air conditioning, a stereo, and double doors in the back. And get a little ramp, so you can drive the forklift into the van, and I can drive it out when I get there."

"Wait a minute. Are you saying what I think you're—?"

"San Diego. Wild Animal Park. Now, just hear me out, okay? I got every detail covered, so just hear me out. At seven forty-five Friday night, you drive up to the zoo's delivery gate in back. You get there by an access road in the park, I'll show you. You drive up to the gate, turn around, park, drive the forklift out, then wait for us to let you in. The three of us go back to the Lion House. Charley's asleep by now. We get the portable cage they got in the storage room. You and Blimp get in Charley's cage, lift him into the portable cage."

"Linda, whoa, wait a minute. He weighs five hundred pounds!"

"Then you *pull* him in, you *push* him in, you *drag* him in! I didn't say it was going to be *easy*. Okay?"

"You realize what could happen if he woke up? I mean, with all the pushing, pulling, dragging, it's possible, right?"

"I'll make sure he gets a strong dose. We'll give him enough to put him out for eight hours."

"You're not a *vet*, Linda. Blimp's not a vet. You don't know how much to give him. That's a five-hundred-pound animal. You can't be *sure* he won't wake up, you know that."

"If he did, if he came to, he'd be too groggy to do anything. And you could be out of there in a flash."

I remember laughing when she said that. More out of fear than anything else. I could visualize myself in that cage with Blimp, pulling Charley's hind legs. You'd really have to see the size of that cat to understand how I was beginning to feel.

Linda could tell. I could see it in her eyes. She lowered her voice, kept it as calm as she could. "After you get him in the portable cage, you lock it, slide it to the edge. Then you'll have to maneuver it onto the pallet of the forklift. And we're home free. Except for one last detail."

"That's it's all a bad dream."

She stared at her cigarette, stubbed it out slowly. "The one last detail is Blimp. He'll have to do what I tell him, because he's not getting the tape or the Polaroids anyway, *ever*. I'll make that clear to him. I'll make it clear that anytime I feel like it, I can send copies to his wife. So, here's the final shot. When we're ready to leave the Lion House, I'll order him to strip and get in the cage."

"Oh, Linda, come on, that's—"

"If he refuses, it's up to you. I'll *depend* on you, Daryll, and it's very important to me. Very important. I want him stripped, and I want him in that empty *cage*. Then I want to *lock* it, myself. I want him to know how that *feels*, to spend the night in there. I have a vivid mental picture of that. I've had it for days now. After we leave, he'll start screaming his lungs out for help. But nobody'll hear him, of course, because the other animals will be roaring and screeching then, too, and those walls are so thick they're practically soundproof. He'll be in competition with those families of baboons and gorillas. Plus the four lions, the leopard, cheetah, panther, the female tiger, all of them. Blimpo Shultz, naked in Charley's cage, screaming with the other animals. Every human being who's oblivious to caged animals should be made to spend time in one of those cages, if only for a night. To see how it feels. To see how it *feels* to be a beautiful wild animal, confined to a little shithole cage all your life, simply because you *exist*.

Not because you've done anything to deserve that kind of punishment. To be punished just because it *entertains* human beings to gawk at you in your misery. Well, at least one oblivious, arrogant scumbag of a human being will get a taste of it. It's not much, but it's better than nothing. And one beautiful animal will finally, finally get a taste of what it's like to run wild in the open. He's only got a year or two to live, but at least he'll get a taste of it. I figure it's only fair that he does."

8

LINDA, ALDO AND I spent Memorial Day out at my parents' home in Jackson Heights, Queens. It was a modest two-story, two-bedroom house on Astoria Boulevard, the same one I'd grown up in, and I always felt a strange sense of security when I was there. I remember it was a warm, hazy afternoon, relatively quiet except for the usual pattern of jets taking off from La Guardia, and Dad barbecued chicken breasts in the backyard. He was fifty-six then, a rugged-looking Irishman who'd been an airline mechanic most of his adult life. He'd always been on the heavy side, he liked his beer, but during the six years he'd been confined to a wheelchair he'd really put on weight. Both legs had been crushed under a jet engine that fell during a routine overhaul. They were permanently and totally useless. The union managed to get him a disability settlement of $200,000 in a lump sum, which was earning good interest, and his company pension—after thirty-four years on the job—was more than adequate even with inflation. So he had no financial problems, at least, and that always gave me a good feeling.

The accident hadn't changed his basic appetite for life, not until recently, but it sure as hell had increased his appetite for beer. I'd say, conservatively, that he was about fifty pounds overweight, and he didn't seem to give a damn anymore. Like, his cheeks and jowls appeared to just bloat down into his shoulders, and his belly started right below his chest and kept going. Somehow, the fat didn't seem to change his face all that much. His gray hair was still full and curly, and beneath the bushy brows, the transparent blue eyes still held the same optimistic twinkle as always. Even his mouth had the same lines, as if set to smile at the slightest provocation.

But according to my mother, he'd been experiencing protracted periods of depression for almost a year then. She couldn't seem to snap him out of it. Before the accident, he'd always spent some time with his buddies down at McGinn's, the local bar, which was just three blocks away, and he still did. But lately he'd been drinking there in the afternoons and not even coming home for dinner. By the time he'd wheel himself back to the house, it would be close to midnight (later on weekends) and he'd be zonked out of his mind. Not only zonked, but abusive. Because of the wheelchair, he slept in the den just off the living room, connected to the kitchen by a short hallway with a bathroom. He'd gotten into the habit of coming home, ignoring the dinner that was left for him, raiding the refrigerator, smashing stuff around, then going into the den and turning the TV up so loud that my mother couldn't possibly sleep through it. She was convinced he did it on purpose to provoke a good argument. And, apparently, they'd been having some lulus lately.

Anyway, that Memorial Day started out well enough and Mother obviously went to a lot of trouble for us. The dining room table was laid with her best linen, silverware and china; the chicken breasts had been marinated in teriyaki sauce; she'd prepared a colorful tossed salad, her special crumb cake for dessert, and even some cheese dips with potato chips, crackers and celery, which we had in the yard while Dad barbecued on the old Weber. He had fixing chicken breasts down to a science. When the coals had been going for at least half an hour, he'd place the breasts on, bone-side down first, put on the lid, cook them for exactly eight minutes, turn them over, then give them another eight minutes. That's all. I'd never known him to screw up marinated chicken breasts, drunk or sober. They came out tender as you please, singed to perfection, with the usual pleasant trace of charcoal.

Unfortunately, during dinner, Aldo and I made the mistake of trying to discuss the sporting goods store with Dad. As I remember it, we were trying to convince him that sporting goods were bigger than ever before, a business with recognized growth potential, and Dad was trying to convince us that we were full of bullshit. I think he'd had only three or four glasses of beer at that point. Every time he said the word bullshit, my mother glared at him. I decided to drop the subject, but Aldo kept up the chatter.

"There's never been a better time," he told Dad.

"Yeah. Particularly with inflation that won't quit and a recession that's deeper than anybody thought it'd be."

"It's bottomed out, Mr. Deever."

"Yeah. That's why interest rates are higher than they've been in ten years. Good thinking."

"It's bottomed out. All the experts—"

"Bullshit."

Mother stopped eating, stared at her plate. She was only a few years younger than Dad, but she'd started to look a lot older during the past year or so. For one thing, she'd started smoking again, after giving them up years ago, and she'd lost weight she couldn't afford to lose. As a result, the lines in her cheeks and neck were more pronounced. Although she'd gone to the hairdresser on Saturday and had a permanent that held well, she'd also had a rinse that made her gray hair seem slightly blue in daylight. But the thing I noticed most was the change in her eyes. They used to be her best feature. I kept glancing at her that afternoon, trying to decide what had happened. All I can say is, almost all the sparkle and mischief were gone. Even when she smiled, her eyes were unhappy.

"We're looking around for a good spot right now," Aldo went on. "I quit my job to look for a good spot. All we need is some money."

Dad took a long swallow of beer. "You got spots in your head, Aldo. All you need is money. What kind of bullshit is that?"

"Oh, c'mon, Dad."

"Don't c'mon me, four-eyes. If you were so smart, you would've got something out of that war. You got your eyes screwed up and didn't get a penny for it. All it would've taken was some form. You could be getting disability right now."

"But I'm not disabled, Dad. I'm just fine."

Linda tried to help. "It's true, Mr. Deever, he's not—"

"Oh, bullshit!"

Mother stood up fast. "I can't take that. I just can't take that anymore. I've had it. I simply can't take that kind of language from you anymore."

Linda and I got up, went over and tried to calm her down. We eased her back into the chair. Then, in the silence that followed, we sat down and looked at her.

Her eyes had filled. "My father was a high school principal and in my family we simply didn't tolerate that kind of—"

"Bullshit!" Dad shouted.

Mother left the table immediately, ran into the living room and up the stairs. Linda started after her, but I grabbed her arm as I stood up, motioned for her to stay, then walked quickly into the living room and up the stairs.

The bedroom door was open. I went in slowly. Mother was standing by the back windows overlooking the yard, crying softly, hands to her face. She looked small and fragile in the dim light from the half-drawn blinds. I cleared my throat quietly to tell her I was there, went over and stood behind her. I put my arms around her. We didn't say anything for what seemed like a long time. I remember the muted sound of voices from downstairs and the tinkle of silverware on china. Finally, Mother wiped her face with the palms of her hands, crossed her arms and held on to my wrists tightly. Her hands were very wet.

"He didn't mean it," I said softly.

She nodded, remained silent.

"He's just had too much to drink."

Her voice was hoarse. "I swear to God, I don't know what it's all about anymore. I'm fifty-two years old and I don't know what it's all about anymore."

"Want to talk about it?"

"Close the door, will you?"

When I closed it quietly and came back, she was leaning against the wall close to the windows, arms folded over her chest, holding herself, as if she were cold. The light from the blinds threw pale stripes across her face. She was looking through the slats and frowning.

"When did you move out?" she asked.

"About two years ago."

She spoke just above a whisper. "He was never like this

before. Never. Not even when you were in Vietnam. When the accident happened, he took it—you remember. He took it so . . . bravely. Bravely is the only word. You were here, you saw him. And now six years have passed. And he's a different person. He's like a stranger sometimes, Daryll. He says things to me that I—wouldn't even repeat to you. That I—don't even want to think about. Hurtful things. Things that hurt very, very deeply. It's like he's drunk most of the time now, like he wants to stay drunk. He said he never should've married me. He said I forced him into it. He said he never really wanted to get married and never wanted a child. He said he's wasted his life now, that it's too late."

"He didn't mean any of that stuff. You know he didn't."

She was crying again, fighting for control. "He said things about you. That you're an emotional cripple. That you'd be content to be a janitor for the rest of your life. That you live in a dream world. I've tried to reason with him, but I can't. I just can't. He's never sober enough to talk sense anymore."

"I'll speak to him. That's a promise. I'll get him sobered up and we'll have a long talk."

"He says he doesn't honestly know what he's supposed to be living for anymore. He hasn't gone to church in—I suppose it's four or five years now. At first, I thought it was the transition, you know, that he'd pull himself together. Then I thought it was the embarrassment of the wheelchair. In front of all his friends. But I was kidding myself. I was making up excuses and closing my mind to the real truth."

I waited. "And what's that?"

She looked at me then, and the bands of light moved on her face. "The truth? The truth is, he just doesn't care anymore. About me, about you, about anybody or anything. The truth is, in the deepest part of him, he thinks he's a failure. He thinks he's failed as a father, because of you, because—forgive me for this."

"Go ahead. Say it."

"Because of the way you turned out."

"All right. Understood."

"I've said, 'Listen, Daryll's only thirty years old, he's got plenty of time to make something of himself.' I've said, 'Listen, he's not content to be a janitor, he has a dream and you can help him. He wants to open that sporting goods store with Aldo, and they need money, and you can help them.' Well, you know your father. It's a dead issue as far as he's concerned. He says he's not about to sink any part of his disability settlement into a pipe dream. He says Aldo's a loser and you don't have sense enough to come in out of the rain. He says to make a pipe dream like that come true, you need somebody with hard-headed business sense, and neither of you have it."

I thought about that, took out a pack of cigarettes, started to light one, then remembered and offered her one. Her hand shook just perceptibly as she took it. I lighted it. She inhaled deeply, blew smoke toward the blinds, watched it move through, bounce off the window and curl upward.

"And he thinks he's failed as a husband," she said quietly. "We haven't lived as husband and wife for—at least five years now. I think it's because he—I don't know. Because he thinks I'm somehow—repelled by him now. And I'm not. God knows, I'm not. I can't say I love him now the way I did when we were young. It's a different kind of love now, Daryll, it's hard to explain. It's much stronger, much deeper than you have when you're young. It's hard to put into words. The right words. When you feel love like I feel for your father, sex isn't important anymore. Sex pales in the presence of love like that. Because it's real. It's solid. Not that the other kind of love is *un*real, but this is something entirely different. This is something that grows from the other kind, if you're lucky. Maybe lucky isn't exactly the right word, but still. I don't know when the transformation happened. Very gradually, I suppose. All I know is, somewhere along the way, as the anniversaries went by, as the unsolvable problems didn't get solved sometimes, but got put in perspective, somewhere down the line I just became aware of the fact that the foundation was so solid it wouldn't be broken. Maybe when you're thirty years old it sounds dumb to hear this, but it was like a discovery. It was like a discovery and it gave me a very calm feeling. Despite everything that life threw at us, we'd made it. We had the real thing that everybody talks about. The kind of thing that kids dream about when they get married."

We listened to the sound of dishes being stacked in the kitchen. After a while, the screen door in back opened, slammed shut and bounced. It opened a second time, stayed open longer before the slam and bounce. We heard Linda's voice, muffled by the window, then my father's, then Aldo's.

Mother gazed out at them, still leaning against the wall, and smiled. "When I first met your father, Daryll, he was really—he was something. We've been married—what?—thirty-two years, so this was thirty-three, almost thirty-four years ago. You've seen pictures of him in uniform, but you can't imagine what he was really like. I remember him so clearly. I was eighteen, younger than Linda even. He was twenty-two. This was the summer of 1946, the year after the war ended. I'd just finished my freshman year at Barnard and my parents had their hearts set on my graduating and going on to graduate school and becoming a teacher. But that summer I started dating this young man named Robert Deever. Bobby Deever, who was still in the Air Force. He was an aircraft mechanic. God, he was handsome. He looked very much like you—tall, blond, strong. Like you looked in uniform, except the Air Force had much snappier outfits."

"Snappier than Marine dress blues? Stop it."

She laughed softly, took a drag on her cigarette, removed it slowly, blew smoke at the ceiling. "My dad didn't like him at all. Said he was too cocky. Bobby Deever drove a brand-new white Ford convertible with red upholstery. And when I went back to Barnard in the fall and lived in Brooks Hall, Mr. Deever drove up there almost every evening. He was on terminal leave, waiting for his discharge, applying to most of the major commercial airlines. And on weekends, we'd go to football games and movies and musicals and out to fancy restaurants. With the top down. And he had money to burn. And he spoiled me rotten. Then he got his discharge and accepted a job with United Airlines and started working at La Guardia. I don't . . . I don't actually remember the first time I realized I was in love. But one Saturday night during Christmas vacation, he took me to the 21 Club. First time we'd ever gone there."

In the pause, we listened to the soft voices from the yard.

"And?" I said.

"You've heard it before. Let's go downstairs."

"Tell me again. Please."

She smiled, shook her head, then frowned, as if trying to remember. "And we sat in candlelight, holding hands. Waiting for our martinis. And he seemed very nervous."

She couldn't continue. We listened to Aldo's voice. He was attaching the garden hose to the outside faucet. I glanced out and saw Dad beginning to water the lawn.

Mother walked to the bedside table, stubbed out her cigarette in the ashtray. "Come on, I've made crumb cake for dessert. It's his favorite."

9

TRUE TO HIS WORD, Aldo went to see Mr. Long himself the next morning, Tuesday, May 27. He'd been warned not to enter the building, so he waited at the main entrance, wearing his best suit, absolutely determined to create the most favorable impression possible, and to apologize in the most sincere way he could muster. He'd even rehearsed the whole thing in his mind and memorized the actual speech. I have all this secondhand from Aldo, of course; I wasn't there. He called me later that morning, woke me up, but I'd asked him to. I was very anxious to hear how it went, and I was optimistic because of the timing.

When Aldo called, his voice was shaking. As nearly as I can recall the disjointed conversation, here's what apparently happened:

At about eight forty-five that morning, Mr. Long and his son were dropped off by their limousine and walked up the steps. Aldo greeted them warmly just outside the entrance and tried to make a good impression by speaking some of the Vietnamese phrases he'd learned during the war, you know, polite stuff, flattering. Well, it didn't work. Mr. Long was just obviously displeased to see him. Before Aldo could even get into his apology, the old man scowled in disgust, muttered something in Vietnamese to his son, and they walked past into the building. Aldo said he was so goddam humiliated and angry he damn near went after them. The sight of the security cop inside stopped him.

Up to that time, I'd been trying to take Long's attitude somewhat philosophically, trying to understand his side of it as best I could. The fact is, he'd always been pleasant to me, the few times I'd spoken with him, and so had his son. And although I hadn't seen the actual cause of the basket scuffle, I'd sure as hell seen Aldo in action with the guy, kicking the stuff at him with a vengeance and calling him every name he could think of. But Long's deliberate rudeness that morning at the entrance really pissed me off. If that's what happened (and I think Aldo told it essentially straight), then maybe all the secondhand stories we'd heard about him in Saigon were really true. Maybe he was a scumbag.

One thing was for damn sure: Aldo could forget about getting his job back. He hadn't worked there nearly long enough to be eligible for unemployment benefits, so I knew he'd be in a financial bind before very long. I told him not to sweat it, that I had a little saved and that I expected him to hit me for whatever he needed. We'd helped each other out like that for years, and it was always strictly on a loan basis, never a gift. Over the past eight years, whenever I was out of work, I'd be into him for at least a couple of hundred before I could start paying him back. That morning we also discussed the idea of his looking for a job in a sporting goods store. We'd both gone that route before, of course, and those jobs were always few and far between, plus they didn't pay well when you could find one, but times were changing. He seemed to pick up a bit at that point. Said he'd get a copy of Sunday's *Times* and today's *Village Voice,* check out anything listed. Said he'd check back with me that afternoon, but I didn't hear from him.

At work that night, I was a little down. The Long incident was a factor, plus I was always kind of down after a big weekend; it took me a while to get back in the full rhythm of the whole routine. On top of that, I hadn't been able to get back to sleep after Aldo's call that morning, so I knew I'd be bushed by the time one o'clock rolled around.

When I got to the second floor that night, Mr. Long's office was the only one lighted, as usual. The only thing different was that his radio was playing, which always meant that one of them had taken off early. Always the same FM station, mood stuff. Wasn't that loud, but I remember how the music sort of echoed in the empty corridor, you know? When I'd finished the floor and was completing my rounds for the trash, old man Long opened the door, placed his two baskets down, nodded and smiled at me as he went inside. I didn't even nod. Just gave him a cold stare.

It was a bitch to work that building alone. Way too much for one man. I decided to call George Fox first thing the next day and ask him to get his ass in gear for Aldo's replacement, or get a temporary guy until he could find somebody. Christ, I'd been working the night shift alone since the previous Tuesday when Aldo got suspended. Anyway, I took about five coffee breaks that night; I figured I deserved them.

At about eleven-thirty, I'd finished all the floors, which wasn't bad, but I hadn't baled any of the trash yet; I'd left it for last. I remember compacting the first bale, hauling it out, filling up the machine again and feeling really tired. So while the machine was pressing the second load, I just stretched out on the wooden bench in the locker room and tried to grab a catnap. Big mistake. Went out like a light.

I woke up very suddenly. I think I'd been having a nightmare or something, because I was sweating and disoriented. Glanced at my watch fast and couldn't believe it; glanced again: five past two. My back was stiff from the bench, and my neck really ached. I'd only fallen asleep on that job once before and swore to myself I'd never do it again. It just pissed me off when I did stuff like that. I felt guilty about it, but I knew I'd had it. I couldn't go back to work then. I didn't take a shower, just washed my hands, took a leak, changed to street clothes and went upstairs.

I remember I was walking through the lobby, fishing for the front-door key, when I heard it: the sound of distant music, almost inaudible. I was so sure it was from the street that I kept walking to the door. Then, standing at the door, I realized it wasn't from outside. It was coming from the open stairway to the second floor. Had to be Mr. Long. For just an instant, I considered locking the front door on the bastard. He didn't have the key; none of the tenants did. It seems crazy, but I tried to visualize him walking down those steps, really exhausted, trying the front door, suddenly realizing he was locked in for the night. Wondered what he'd do. Probably call George Fox at home, get him out of bed. No way. Then I thought: Shit, the jerk's probably fallen asleep up there. I looked at the wall clock: two-fifteen. Had to smile. Go up, bang on his door, embarrass the piss out of him. Never have a better opportunity.

I walked up the stairway, opened the exit door. It was his radio, all right, mood music echoing, but louder than before. The window in his door threw a warm yellow rectangle on the buffed floor. I went up and knocked on the door, much louder than necessary, raised my voice so he'd know I was pissed off.

"I have to lock up now."

No reply. I knocked again, even harder.

"Mr. Long?"

Nothing. I went through my keys, unlocked his door and opened it just wide enough to yell his name again, but I never got a word out. The right side of his office looked like it'd been ransacked. File-cabinet drawers were open, jewel boxes were scattered around, papers were all over the floor. There was a strong smell of urine in the room. I opened the door wider, glanced to my left. Unfortunately, the memory of what I saw then will be frozen in my mind for as long as I live.

Mr. Long's thin body was slumped in a chair, one foot jammed into a trash basket. His face was dark-blue, his eyes wide. His left hand clutched his throat, and several cut and bleeding fingers had managed to get under the wire that was wrapped tightly around his neck. Inches above the floor, his right hand held a knife with pale traces of blood on it. I don't know how long I stood there and stared at him. I remember feeling almost paralyzed, hearing the loud music, aware of my fast breathing, my heart pounding like crazy. At some point, the telephone began ringing and seemed to snap me out of it. My first instinct was to run, then I took a deep breath and tried to concentrate. The telephone kept ringing. My left hand was still on the doorknob. The smell of urine made me feel suddenly dizzy. I backed out of the office, closed the door, started toward the stairs. Then I went back, took out a handkerchief and wiped the doorknob very carefully.

I wiped the knob of the stairway exit door on both sides. It wasn't until I was walking down the stairs that I realized the killer was undoubtedly still in the building. He couldn't get out without a key. He could be down in the lobby. I went down the last few steps very softly, close to the left wall, knowing he wouldn't stand near the front of the lobby. I stopped at the foot of the stairs, listened for maybe ten or fifteen seconds. My arms and legs were still shaking. All I could hear was the faint sound of the radio. Staying against the wall, I looked around the corner toward the other end of the lobby; I always kept half the lights on all night, per our building security instructions. I could only see the straight corridor itself, of course, not the series of wings holding the elevators. I went to the front door quickly, unlocked it, slipped outside, locked it again fast. Sweat was dripping down my face. I took one last look inside. Nothing.

Then I actually ran down the steps and over to my cycle. I had trouble finding the key to the rear-wheel lock. When I jumped on and got the engine started, I squealed it away, jumped the curb, crossed the street, headed north on Sixth, and one car passed me almost immediately, going the wrong way on the one-way street; the driver had his brights on and momentarily blinded me. That was the one and only car on that particular section of Sixth at that time of morning, and whoever it was got a damn good look at me driving away from the building.

I turned right on Forty-second, by habit, and made the decision that I had to talk with my father immediately. By that time, getting some fresh air in my lungs, I knew I should never have left the scene, it was really dumb, the worst move I could've made. If I'd been thinking straight,

I would've locked myself in Long's office, called the police, then called George Fox to let them in. But what can I tell you? I was scared shitless. That's the plain, simple truth. Now I was in serious trouble. The only person I was absolutely certain I could depend on for advice and help was my father.

About half an hour later I was tooling along in the middle lane of the Long Island Expressway when I heard a siren behind me. I glanced in my left rear-view mirror and saw the flashing lights of a police car coming up on me fast. First thing, I looked at my speedometer. I was under the speed limit, but traffic was very light that time of morning and there was no question who they were after. I remember how my whole frame of mind changed in those seconds, like I was coming to my senses for the first time. As I hit my directional signal and headed for the far-right lane, I actually felt relieved. I decided the whole thing had gone far enough, I'd tell the truth right now before I got in any deeper. I mean, what the hell was I running for? I hadn't done anything. Okay, right, I'd left the scene of a major crime, I'd admit that flat out, but that was it, I wasn't guilty of anything else. And they couldn't prove anything else. When I reached the right lane and slowed to pull off the road, the police car killed its siren and just drove alongside on my left. The cop in the passenger seat leaned out, pointed to his head, smiled and waved a finger at me. I'd forgotten to put on my helmet. I nodded that I understood and tried to smile back. They killed the flashing lights and pulled away.

I was shaking like a son of a bitch. I stopped, got off fast, kicked the stand, started swearing at myself. My helmet, gloves and a few tools were in a little black metal case mounted on the rear behind the passenger seat. As I was trying to unlock it in the semidarkness, my hands were shaking like I had palsy. I remember taking a deep breath and thinking: What the hell am I *doing* here? Why the hell am I *running?* What the hell am I *afraid* of?

I arrived at my parents' house at three twenty-five and the place was dark, of course, its white wooden shingles bathed in the glow of the streetlamp out front. There were houses on either side, and I didn't want to wake anybody up, so I shut off the engine in the street and wheeled the cycle into our driveway. I unlocked the front door quietly, went directly to the kitchen and turned on the small lamp on the counter rather than the overhead lights. When I walked down the hall toward the den, I could see Dad dimly in the light from the kitchen, already awake, propped up on his elbows.

"What the hell's going on?"

"I'm sorry, Dad. I need your advice."

"My *advice!* What the hell *time* is it?"

"About three-thirty."

"Are you out of your *head!*"

"Sorry, Dad. I'm in trouble."

He blinked rapidly. "What kind of trouble?"

"Serious."

"Help me up. Get me on the couch."

I carried him over to the couch, turned on a couple of lamps and made us both some instant coffee. My mother called downstairs and I assured her everything was okay, told her to go back to sleep. Then we settled down and I explained everything that'd happened, as clearly and honestly as I could. He remained silent through most of it, nodding, trying to understand it from my point of view. When he was sure I'd told the whole story, he asked questions in his husky voice.

"Why should you feel guilty?"

I shrugged. "It's just that I wasn't supposed to be in the building at that hour."

"Why were you in the building that late? Tell me again."

"I just fell asleep."

He nodded, rubbed his hand over the stubble on his cheek. "There's an alibi only a mother would love."

"It's not an alibi."

"I'll say it's not. You were asleep—at home. If it comes out you were there in the building, you either look like a suspect to the cops or a witness to whoever killed Long. Or both." He hesitated, considering something. "I assume you had nothing to do with it."

"Oh, c'mon, Dad."

"Don't c'mon me, four-eyes." He smiled then, just a slight upturn at the corners of his mouth. "All right, you're in the clear. So stay in the clear. You're alive. So stay alive. Keep your mouth shut."

That's what he said.

10

I WAS IN MY APARTMENT when the police called at ten thirty-five that morning. I was still awake—I hadn't had any sleep at all since returning from Queens at about five—but I let the phone ring four times before answering, then tried to sound like I'd been awakened. A man who identified himself as Lieutenant Jacobs, Midtown Precinct South, homicide division, explained that I was wanted for routine questioning in a homicide that had taken place in the Waring Building, and told me to meet him as soon as possible in office 221, occupied by a firm called Long & Son. He suggested that I enter the building through the rear door to avoid questioning by the press out front. That's all. Well, I'd been expecting the call for hours, I'd showered and shaved, had breakfast, everything. My eyes looked like hell and I'd tried putting drops in them, but it didn't seem to help much. I was just plain exhausted. I was also extremely tense. I considered taking maybe five milligrams of Valium, but in my condition I thought even that amount might put me to sleep. I took two aspirin instead, then had another cup of coffee and tried to settle down before leaving about eleven. I took my time driving up there.

Cops were all over the building, even at the rear entrance. I had a slight hassle with one of them standing outside Long's office, finally had to show him identification before he'd let me in. Arrogant bastard, too, like he was doing me a favor. God, I hate cops like that. Another cop was inside the door, and he was just the opposite. Pointed out Lieutenant Jacobs for me, spoke very politely. First thing I noticed was that everything had been cleaned up; they must've been working in there all morning. George Fox was in the office of Long's son, talking with Bill Johnson and one of the janitors from the day shift.

Lieutenant Jacobs looked almost as tired as me, sitting sideways at one of the little desks in the area to the right of Mr. Long's office, tie pulled down, suit coat open. He was a heavyset Jewish guy, early forties, receding hair, hard mouth. His badge was on a leather backing that was clipped to the breast pocket of his coat. He shook hands, thanked me for coming, asked me to take a chair. As I did, his partner came out of Long's office, glanced at me, then leaned against the doorframe, a tall, slim black guy with a mustache and short afro, younger than Jacobs, looking relaxed in an open sport shirt and jacket.

Jacobs asked me a couple of questions about myself before I had a chance to ask him who was killed.

"Man by the name of Nyen Long," he told me. "Sorry, I assumed you knew by now."

I shook my head. "When was he killed?"

"Apparently last night."

"In here?"

"Apparently. What're your hours?"

"Five in the afternoon till one in the morning."

He nodded, shooed a fly away. "I understand from Mr. Fox that you worked alone last night."

"Yes, sir."

"When you worked this floor, was Mr. Long still here?"

"Yes, sir."

"Are you certain?"

"Yes, sir. He put out his trash baskets, same as always."

"You saw him do that?"

"Yes, sir."

"What time was that?"

"I'm not sure of the exact time, but I'd—"

"Approximately."

"I'd say it was about six, six-fifteen, something like that."

"And it was definitely Mr. Long, not his son?"

"No, sir, it was the older man."

"He say anything to you?"

"No, sir, just smiled and nodded."

"I see. Now, as I understand it from Mr. Fox, you have

a master key and you usually go into the offices for the trash baskets. Correct?"

"That's correct."

"How come Mr. Long put his baskets outside? Why was that?"

I shrugged. "He usually worked late. I guess he didn't want us coming in the office."

"So he always followed the same routine about it?"

"Yes, sir. Actually, his son usually put the baskets out."

"You say he usually worked late? How late?"

"I don't really know that. They're usually still working when I go to the next floor."

"Was his son with him last night?"

"I don't know for sure. I only saw the older man."

The black cop got into it then, still leaning against the doorframe. "What time did you lock up last night?"

"One o'clock, as always. I assumed the building was empty."

"You didn't hear anything?"

"Hear anything? No, sir."

He nodded. "The name's Lieutenant Black. That should be easy to remember. You a vet?"

"Yes."

"You know Allan Mercer?"

"Aldo? Sure. We were in Vietnam. We've been buddies ever since."

"Both of you Marines?"

"No. Ex-Marines."

Jacobs' chair squeaked as he leaned forward. "Did you know Long when you were in Vietnam?"

"No, but I knew *of* him. Everybody did. Both sides thought he was working for them. He bought and sold everything, including information, and got paid by everybody involved. Even the Russians were paying him to snoop on his own allies. At least, that's how the rumor went."

Jacobs thought about that, then seemed to choose his words very carefully. "I would think, if that were true, you'd have a grudge a mile long."

"I would think *you* would, too. It wasn't just *my* country, was it?"

He hadn't expected that. I remember how he blinked,

then shifted to another subject quickly. "Why was Aldo fired?"

I hesitated, tried to think of the right way to put it.

"We know why he was fired," Black said. "Did he ever show up here after he was dismissed?"

"Not that I know of."

"You working tonight?" Jacobs asked.

"I expect to."

Black frowned, looked at me closely. "You better go home then and get some sleep. Looks like you didn't get much sleep last night."

"It was hot."

He nodded. "It's going to get hotter, they say. If you don't want to talk to the reporters, you go out the back way."

"Right, thank you." I stood up, smiled, walked between them to the door. The cop standing there opened it for me.

A small group of Vietnamese had gathered out in the hall then, apparently waiting to go in for questioning. Long's son was among them, wearing a black suit. He was comforting an old woman dressed in black, probably his mother. As the door closed, they all stopped talking and looked at me. I mean, they looked at me hard. Gave me a very strange feeling. The expression in their eyes reminded me instantly of the war. I turned away quickly, started walking. When I'd almost reached the stairway, they started talking again.

I'd planned to go straight back to the apartment, call Dad and tell him how it went, then maybe grab a few hours of sleep before work. As I reached the lobby, I started to turn left and head for the back door, but I was curious to see the TV crews on the steps out front; I'd caught a fast glimpse of them when I arrived. So I turned around and looked. I often wonder what would've happened if I hadn't done that. The door to the right of the revolving doors, the one I used to get out every night, held a big rectangle of glass that was separated by two horizontal steel bars, used to push the door open, and in the lower half, framed as if on television, I saw the head and shoulders of Tony Sokolow. She was standing down on the steps talking to her cameraman. It was the first time I'd ever seen her in person. For just a couple of seconds,

I couldn't believe it was her. I walked closer to the door fast, took another look. It was her. Obviously, she was subbing for somebody that day. She held a mike with the big number 5 on it and was flanked by a guy with an RCA videotape camera mounted on his shoulder and a sound technician.

Well, I knew I had to go out and take a good look at her, a long look. I hesitated, glanced at the other TV crews. Practically all the local channels were represented, you could see the numbers on the mikes. They were all just standing around, talking, waiting to interview somebody. Then I thought: Christ, if I go through that door, every TV crew out there will probably rush me, I'll be mobbed. I glanced at my clothes. I was wearing a plaid sport shirt, old denim Levi's, and carrying my leather jacket and helmet. Not too impressive, right? Well, I thought, so what? At least I'd get to see Tony, maybe close up. Maybe I'd even get to talk with her. Talk with her? Hell, I'd give her an exclusive.

I took a fast swipe at my hair, adjusted my glasses, cleared my throat, walked out the door and braced for the rush. Nothing. A few reporters and cameramen glanced up at me, then returned to their conversations. Actually, to tell you the truth, I was very relieved. I was nobody again, the way I liked it. I walked down toward Tony, slowly, nervously. At that point, she was still talking to her cameraman, but her back was turned to me. Probably hadn't even seen me, which was fine with me. When I got down to the step she was standing on, I wasn't that close, maybe five feet away. I glanced around casually as I moved closer to her. Finally, I was standing directly behind her. I took deep breaths. I really didn't know my next move. I think I just wanted to be close to her, to get a good look at her. Dumb, I know. I remember she was taller than I expected, wore a simple, neatly tailored red outfit with three-quarter sleeves, and I could see the collar of her white blouse. Standing that close, I could even catch traces of her perfume. I must've been staring, because when I glanced up at the cameraman, he was giving me a funny look. Tony noticed and turned around to face me.

"Yes?" she said.

I swear to God, she was even better-looking than on

television. She seemed much younger. I just didn't know what to say. I remember her face vividly, but I don't recall what I said. I think I blurted out something like, "Uh, Lieutenant Black said that I'm supposed to talk with reporters . . . and I guess you're it."

She frowned slightly, exchanged a glance with her cameraman.

I realized she needed more bait. "I'm the night janitor in the building here."

That did it. Her eyes darted to the other TV crews fast, then back at me. She leaned close, kept her voice very low. "We'll meet you at the back of the building. Don't talk to anyone else, okay?"

I nodded, walked slowly down the steps. I felt like I was on a real high. I turned the corner, walked toward the back of the building. I remember I kept visualizing her face, up close, as she turned around. I felt like running, you know? I felt like jumping. I felt like yelling. I started to laugh, very low at first, then a little louder, the kind of laugh you laugh when you're a child, the kind that comes from down in your stomach. I was so goddam excited I felt like throwing my helmet up in the air as hard as I could. My eyes began to water. I had to say something, to let it out, so I said: "Hot *damn.* Hot *damn!*" I mean, people on the street gave me looks. Here I am, thirty years old, walking down a crowded New York street laughing and swearing out loud to myself, okay? Not that it's that unusual in this town, but you see somebody acting like that on the street, you take it for granted they've more or less blown their doors, right? I didn't even care. I'd never done it before, but I honestly didn't give a shit, I looked people right in the face and kept laughing. That's how zonked I was.

When I got to the rear of the building, I was so anxious to get started, I thought I'd piss my pants or something. I ran up to the glass doors, looked at my reflection, smoothed my hair down, tucked in my shirt, tried to think of what I'd say during my interview. I knew I had to get the point across that I was more than just a janitor. Not that I was ashamed of it; that's what I was and I'd tell her flat out, but I also wanted to fill her in on other things. Of course, I'd never been on television before in my life, and the thought crossed my mind that I'd choke, especially with Tony standing there looking at me, but the idea was so horrible I just blanked it out.

If you want the truth, I did feel butterflies when Tony and her two guys finally got there. They were all business, no small talk, not even a smile. Fast light-meter readings, sound levels, two-shot positioning against the side of the building. Just before we began, I noticed tiny beads of perspiration on Tony's forehead and above her lips. She didn't look calm like on television, at least not yet; she looked very intense and eager. I tried not to stare. I remember her jacket was cut to a V in front, and although the narrow collar of her blouse was white, the rest of it had a delicate pattern of colorful little flowers. It suited her perfectly.

She didn't warn me when they started to shoot. The cameraman just said, "Rolling," the sound technician said, "Speed," and when I realized we were on, my arms and legs started shaking. Tony's reaction was the exact opposite. Almost instantly, she appeared calm again, like she'd flipped a switch in her mind. She lifted the mike, looked directly into the lens, as usual, and her voice had the familiar conversational tone:

"We're talking with a gentleman who works the night shift as a maintenance supervisor—"

"I'm really a janitor," I heard myself say.

"—in the building in which Nyen Long was killed." She turned, tilted the mike toward me. "His name is . . ."

"My name is Daryll Deever." My voice was shaking. For some reason I can't explain, I just kept talking, saying absolutely nothing, looking in her eyes: "I've had this job for about two years. It's a nice job. It's quiet. I'm on my own. I like that. I'm thirty years old. I have—"

"Well, thank you for that rather lengthy introduction."

I nodded, continued to stare at her, felt the sweat drip.

"What do you know about the murder of Mr. Long?"

"Nothing. I just found out about it."

She hesitated. "Then why are we having this interview?"

"Since you asked me, I'll tell you. I've had a crush on you for over six months. I can't say that I've—"

"Cut!" she said, turning away, dropping her hands to her sides. "Wipe it, Hank." She waited a couple of seconds, as if trying to control herself, then looked at me coldly. "Are you really a maintenance guy in this building?"

I nodded.

"Do you know anything about the murder?"

"What if I did? Maybe I . . ." Fortunately, I stopped myself.

She walked toward the two men, wound up the cord of the mike. "Man, where do they come from?"

"The woodwork," one of them said.

"Let's get back fast," she told them. "Cut through the lobby."

As they walked quickly toward the door, she looked back at me. Not an angry look, not even cold, just curious, frowning slightly. I glanced down at the helmet and jacket in my hands. I could feel blood rushing to my head. I felt embarrassed, sure, but it went far deeper than that. I remember I actually felt dirty standing there, like what I'd said was dirty. To this day, I don't really know why I said all that stuff. I'm sure there's an explanation, I'm sure some psychiatrist could explain behavior like that, give it a neat label and all, but the only excuse I can think of is that maybe I experienced shock. Maybe the reality of Tony standing there talking to me was too much. I know how that sounds, but I'm trying to approach the thing logically. I'm not a mental case, not in the accepted sense, and I never have been. All I know is that the line between fantasy and reality in my mind back then wasn't always clearly defined. Seeing Tony in person for the first time that day was something of a shock in itself, but getting close to her, talking with her, then doing a television interview with her, I suspect that was a case of too much reality too soon.

Anyway, I stood there until they were inside the door, then started walking slowly around the building to get my cycle and go home. When I got around to the front and started unlocking my rear wheel, I heard a lot of commotion on the front steps, looked up and saw Jacobs and Black coming out of the building and being quickly surrounded by the TV crews. Tony and her two guys were right in the thick of it. Jacobs seemed to do most of the talking as they made their way down the steps to their car.

In the midst of all that, I heard Aldo's voice yelling my name. He'd just come out of the front door and was running down the steps toward me. From the time I'd discovered Long's body, I'd made a conscious effort to put Aldo out of my mind, because the thoughts I had bothered the hell out of me. He was my best friend, we'd shared a lot together, and I just didn't want to deal with those thoughts. I had enough problems of my own.

Actually, I had to smile at the asshole, running down the steps in his good suit, grinning like he'd just hit a grand slam in the bottom of the ninth. When he reached me, he was out of breath and laughing.

"Hey, Daryll, you killed the bastard, huh? It was you, right?"

I glanced over at the TV crews. We were too far away to be overheard, but I didn't like it. "Hey, don't. All right?"

He smiled, lowered his voice. "Somebody got him. Whoever it was deserves a medal, man. A medal. Good thing I was at Linda's last night. They thought it was *me!* The cops! The black one especially."

I was so relieved I didn't know what to say.

"Wish I *had* done it," he said softly. "Come on, aren't you sort of glad he got it?"

I shrugged. My eyes went to the windows of Long's office; the sun's reflection put a glare on the glass.

Aldo threw his arm around my shoulders. "Hey, listen, there's a big poker game at Harry's this afternoon. Can you spot me a fifty? I feel lucky today. I feel real lucky."

I took out my wallet, gave him two twenties and a ten. That left me with exactly three dollars, but I didn't give a shit. After what he'd said, I would've gladly given him a check for every dime I had in the bank, and thrown in my cycle to boot.

Late that afternoon, the New York *Post* gave the story a good chunk of space on page three, complete with a formal studio shot of Long and a candid shot of Jacobs and Black being interviewed on the steps of the building. Needless to say, murders in New York happen on a daily basis. Tabloids like the *Post* and the *News* frequently give them prominent space, depending on who was killed, who was involved, and how bizarre it was, but only rarely will a murder make the front page these days, cop killings being a notable exception. As a general rule, papers like the *Times* bury all but the most noteworthy murders in the back. In this case, the *Post* highlighted the fact that Long was not only a wealthy diamond merchant, but was alleged to be a major financial intermediary in high-level diplomatic transactions with the Soviet Union and the South Vietnamese Provisional Revolutionary Government in the illegal "cash for freedom" refugee traffic from those countries to the United States. Wealthy Jewish and Vietnamese groups in the U.S. were believed to have been dealing with Long for years in arranging exit visas for refugees. Therefore, the assumption on the part of the *Post* was that Long's murder was possibly linked to those activities and would probably result in a significant, if temporary, decline in that refugee market. However, no motive or suspects had been revealed by the police.

I wanted to follow the case as closely as possible, of course, so I decided to buy the early editions of the *Times* and *News* when I finished work that night, then go straight home and watch the ten-o'clock news on my video cassette. The more I knew about the facts, the more intelligently I could anticipate and react to the police.

Most of all, I wanted a chance to think, and that night at work was the first real opportunity I had to reflect about exactly what had happened, calmly, quietly, logically, and at considerable length. Now that I knew for sure that Aldo wasn't involved, I tried to put the facts in some kind of perspective. For example, I tried to put myself in the place of the killer. I knew there was no way he could've gotten out of the building that night without a key. So, whether I liked it or not, I had to conclude that he was inside the building when I discovered the body. For all I knew, he might still have been in Long's office when I walked in, or in the darkened corridor outside. When I'd walked through the lobby at two-fifteen, I'd changed to street clothes and was wearing leather boots instead of sneakers, so he undoubtedly heard me, especially when I went up the stairs, banged on Long's door and shouted at him. It wasn't easy to accept, but the only logical assumption was that the killer knew I was there. So, obviously, he knew I was the night janitor. Which meant that he knew my name by now, of course, and my address. I was right in the phone book.

The unanswered question was simple: Did he believe that I'd seen him? It was a question he'd have to deal with quickly. Again, I tried to put myself in his place. I hate to admit this to myself or anyone else, but I'm afraid I'd be the kind of killer who'd leave nothing to chance. Not when my life was at stake. If I thought there was even a remote possibility that someone had caught a glimpse of me, I'd go after him. What would I have to lose? Therefore, I decided to assume that the killer would do the same. The moment I made that decision, I felt more alone than ever before in my life. The fact is, there was no one to turn to, not really, certainly not the police. Not even Aldo. How do you protect someone from the unknown? I knew that every move I made from that time on would have to be consciously defensive. I felt more frightened than I'd ever imagined I could feel.

Strangely, I didn't feel afraid in the building that night. I figured, if I were the killer, that would be the very last place I'd choose to go after the guy. I'd be thinking paranoid, because it was excellent defense: If the night janitor had seen me and told, the police would never reveal that information to anybody, they'd try to anticipate. They'd set up a sophisticated surveillance operation with the witness as bait, totally alone in the building and obviously defenseless. No way. I'd never go near that building. In fact, I'd never go near the witness until I'd checked him out thoroughly, his apartment, his transportation, his routes, his hangouts, his friends, his daily and weekend routines. First, to see if he had undercover protection; and, if not, to determine precisely when and where he was most vulnerable. Make no mistake, that's how a killer would think.

Still, I didn't go out for lunch that night. The truth is, I had absolutely no appetite. I remember sitting in the locker room, drinking coffee and thinking about Tony. In all the excitement of meeting her, talking with her, actually being interviewed by her, I'd almost told her the truth about what I'd seen that night. I couldn't believe I'd been that dumb. But I had. I'd come very close to telling her. I tried to remember the way she turned and looked back at me just before entering the lobby. What was the expression on her face? Not anger, not coldness, not indifference. Curiosity? Had that been it? Had she seen something in my eyes when I hesitated?

Had she listened to what I didn't say?

11

WHEN I LEFT THE BUILDING that night and walked down the steps, it was difficult to believe that not even twenty-four hours had passed since I discovered Long's body. Despite what I'd reasoned about the workings of a killer's mind, I was extremely apprehensive. Tired, very tired, but nervous enough to take a careful look around, and I knew I'd probably be doing that for a long time to come. I'd locked up on time, it was just past one o'clock, and Sixth Avenue wasn't nearly as deserted as it had been at two-thirty the previous morning. Starting my cycle, switching on the single headlight, I remembered the lone car that had passed me with its brights on, going the wrong way. And, for the first time, I wondered: Could that have been him? Would he have waited outside all that time, knowing I hadn't left the building yet, realizing something was wrong? Watching the lighted lobby to see if I'd hear the music and go upstairs? Waiting for me to come down, seeing me run down the steps in panic? And, as he watched me sweat the rear-wheel lock, could he have been calculating the zero to five- or ten-second first-gear speed he'd need to do the job then and there? No. No, that couldn't have been him. How the hell would he have gotten out of the building without a key?

I was anxious to get up to one of the all-night newsstands on Forty-second, buy the early editions, then head straight home and watch the news. When I pulled away in the light traffic, I thought my eyes were playing tricks on me because of the fatigue. I thought I saw Tony Sokolow on the southeast corner of Forty-first, trying to hail a taxi. It was a girl who looked very much like her. As I approached the corner, I flipped up the plastic visor on my helmet and took a better look. For the second time that day, I experienced a feeling close to shock. It was her. It was Tony, wearing exactly the same outfit, standing just out from the curb, squinting, looking down Sixth, arm raised to flag a cab. She was oblivious to me when I slowed down. In fact, she didn't even turn to look at me until I stopped.

She didn't seem to recognize me in the helmet and jacket. Then a look of surprise came over her face. She gave me a cool smile. Well, I was very, very excited, but I tried to match that coolness.

"Want a lift?"

She glanced at the cycle uneasily. "No, thank you. I should get a cab any second now."

"Come on, it's really comfortable. I'll go slow."

She smiled, shook her head, glanced down Sixth.

"Take you right to your door. Scout's honor."

"I'm afraid it's a long ride."

"Where to?"

"West Fourteenth. Between Fifth and Sixth."

"I live on West Fourth! Hop on!"

She laughed softly, took one last look down the avenue, shrugged, walked back to climb aboard. "Your first name's Daryll, I remember that."

"Deever. Daryll Deever."

She got on a little awkwardly. "Should've worn jeans, right?"

"You'll be fine. Got enough room?"

"Plenty."

"Okay, hang onto my waist. It's the only way."

"Check."

Well, I mean, what can I tell you? I don't even know how to begin. When her arms came around and tightened, my arms and legs started to shake almost immediately. One thing, I was so tired, I didn't really trust my feelings anymore. So much had happened that day, it was like I was observing somebody else's emotions, okay? Guys like me didn't have stuff like this happen to them. That's no shit, that's straight. We don't even expect stuff like this to happen. But it was happening. Before she could change her mind, I revved the engine fast, flipped my visor down, blasted away, then slowed instantly when I remembered. As I turned east on Forty-second and headed for Fifth, I felt that incredible sensation of being sky-high again. Zonked. Yeah! Felt the laughter coming from deep down. Gritted my teeth. Felt like yelling something, hollering something, letting it out. Knew I couldn't. Turning south on Fifth, all the traffic lights were red as far down as I could see; then, after another block, they were all green, a long string of green in the night, and I felt a terrific urge to kick that cycle hard, to tear-ass down Fifth like a cowboy. Then I thought: Christ, that's why you blew it with her this morning. You were thinking of yourself, not her. You were coming on so strong, you would've turned off a cloistered nymph. Cool it. Calm it. Show her you mean what you say.

And I did. Not only that, I enjoyed it. I drove very slowly and enjoyed every minute of it. Know why? That gave me more time with her. Maybe twice as much time, counting the traffic lights I didn't try to beat. And I kept thinking: That's Tony Sokolow right behind you, man. Not the fantasy Tony, the real thing. You can feel her arms around your waist, right? That's no fantasy. Maybe she's never been on a cycle before, ever think of that? Maybe she's a little scared the first time, particularly with you. So think of that. Think of her feelings. For the love of sweet Jesus, don't blow it this time. You're going to find out exactly where she lives. Maybe even get invited up for a nightcap, who knows? Who knows, the way this crazy day is going, anything seems possible. And it did, too. Anything seemed possible.

When I turned slowly into Fourteenth Street, she pointed out her apartment building. It was on our side, north, so I just eased it over, stopped, stood up to steady the cycle as she climbed off. Then I shut off the engine. The apartment was a big, expensive-looking converted brownstone, which made me feel happy. I flipped up my visor.

"Your floors need buffing or something?"

She smiled as she smoothed her skirt. "No."

"I'm real good. A pro. First, I strip the old wax. Then

I lay down an even, smooth coat. Then I buff it, and buff it slowly, gently, till it beams."

"I'm not much for housekeeping. I'm a reporter. Story comes first."

"What comes second?"

"Depends how good the story is."

"That's the curse of being Irish. Women just love me for my stories. You ever have any free time?"

"Free? No. Well, Thursdays. No, I go horseback riding then. I guess not." She smiled warmly then. "Goodnight. Thank you."

"Goodnight," I said softly. "You're welcome."

I kept an eye on her until she was all the way inside. Then I just continued straight past Sixth, hung a left at Seventh, cruised down to West Fourth as if I didn't have a care in the world. I don't know whether Tony had triggered a massive flow of adrenaline or what, but I felt wide awake and full of energy. After parking the cycle and locking it up, I bought the early editions of the papers at the little newsstand in Sheridan Square, looked them over as I walked home. All three papers carried the story, but the *News* gave it five columns.

I felt so charged up when I got home that I really gave Ralph his money's worth. We must've wrestled and rolled around at least twice as long as normal. After that, I couldn't wait to see the news. I rewound the video cassette to the very beginning of the ten-o'clock news and settled back to watch for Tony. I knew they wouldn't run my fiasco interview, of course, but I was hoping she'd managed to get an exclusive with somebody else that day, maybe Jacobs or Black, or even Long's son. As it turned out, the murder was the lead story in the metropolitan area and Tony was seen in two short segments out of five.

First, she appeared with the group of reporters surrounding Jacobs and Black as they walked down the steps of the Waring Building toward their car. There was a lot of jostling for position and Tony held her own, but the guys from CBS, NBC and ABC just had louder voices; Tony didn't get any questions heard. Still, the camera angle was good and she was right in the middle of it all, using her elbows with the best of them. I made an audio tape of all five segments later on, so I could play them next day without the distractions of film. Here's a verbatim transcription of the first:

Reporter: Lieutenant Jacobs, have you any idea as to the value of the stolen diamonds?

Jacobs: No idea.

Reporter: Do you think it was just a robbery?

Black: A robbery took place, yes.

Reporter: Is the FBI being called in?

Jacobs: Why should they be called in?

Reporter: Everybody knows Mr. Long had Russian connections.

Jacobs: Uh-huh, well, that's—

Reporter: Isn't it true that he had friends in high places?

Jacobs: I don't think this was the work of one of his friends.

Reporter: Are there any suspects?

Jacobs: No, we don't have any suspects.

At that point, they climbed into the car and were driven away. I had to smile at those guys. Whatever they knew, the press would never get it out of them. The anchorman narrated a brief introduction to the next segment, saying that Metro News had obtained exclusive interviews with several of Mr. Long's friends and associates, and that the following film had been shot with a concealed camera and microphone at the office of Mr. Chen Bin, a prominent Vietnamese merchant in Chinatown. They started with a long shot of a busy street in Chinatown, then cut to a medium shot of Tony knocking on an office door without a visible mike. The door opened only far enough to reveal the face of an elderly Vietnamese man, and the camera immediately zoomed in on him.

Sokolow: Hello, Mr. Bin. My name is Antonia Sokolow from Metro News. You were a friend of Mr. Long's in Saigon, were you not?

Bin: Mr. Long had many friends.

Sokolow: You were an associate of his for a while, were you not?

Bin: Mr. Long had many associates.

Sokolow: It's true, isn't it, that he was involved in "freedom for cash" for the Vietnamese refugees? Have you any idea what his death means to them?

Bin: Mr. Long is not dead.

Sokolow: Are you saying that the wrong man was killed?

Bin: No, right man was killed. But Mr. Long is not dead. Mr. Long has a son. Son is Mr. Long now.

Tony wasn't involved in the next two interviews, but they were very much like that one in the sense that none of Long's friends would reveal anything new or substantive. Then a spokesman for the office of the chief medical examiner (New York's version of a coroner) stated what was already in the papers, that the cause of death had been confirmed as strangulation; the murder weapon had been a commercial variety of steel wire such as that used in picture framing.

I didn't take Ralph for his walk that night. My energy level began to fall as rapidly as it had risen. After dinner I studied the newspaper stories closely, cut them out, rewound the video cassette to the beginning of the ten-o'clock news and tape-recorded all five segments on the Long story. I double-checked the locks on the door and windows, went to bed early, had a lot of trouble getting to sleep.

Finally, I sat up in bed, had a cigarette and thought about Tony. I'd been so excited about our meeting that night, I hadn't really given much thought to the circumstances. I got up, turned on the light, grabbed the telephone book and looked up the address of Metro News. It was listed under its call letters, WNEW-TV, and the only address listed was 655 Third Avenue. That was somewhere up around Forty-second Street, probably the executive office. Metro was an independent local station; I doubted that they had the actual broadcasting studio there. As I remembered it, most of the TV studios were on the West Side, Sixth and Seventh avenues, roughly Forty-second to maybe Fifty-seventh streets. Well, okay, but why would Tony be at Sixth and Forty-first at about one o'clock in the morning? The ten-o'clock news was a half-hour show and her segments were taped anyway. Then I thought: You're getting seriously paranoid, you know that? She could've been there for any number of completely logical reasons.

Unfortunately, I could think of only one.

12

HORSEBACK RIDING IN MANHATTAN is easy to arrange if you have the bread. You simply call old reliable Claremont Riding Academy at 175 West Eighty-ninth and pick your time. According to the lady I talked with in the office, they're open from six in the morning till six-thirty at night on weekdays. Claremont has a total of sixty horses, but you don't select one, they do, depending on your riding experience. Of course, if you're a "regular," as I found out Tony Sokolow was, you can usually get your favorite horse, and hers was among the best in the stable, a beautiful brown gelding named Prince. She rode him every Thursday from noon until two.

The next Thursday, May 29, I got up early, took Fred for a walk and bought enough carrots to fill one side of the saddlebags I sometimes carry on my cycle. I put a thermos of coffee in the other, drove up to Claremont at eleven-thirty, and learned the riding routes by following a couple of riders, at a discreet distance so I wouldn't spook the horses with my engine. Eighty-ninth is westbound, so they went up to Amsterdam, then north to Ninetieth, east past Columbus, and entered the riding trails at Central Park West. That was up near the enormous Receiving Reservoir, and the trails were really excellent, made of finely crushed cinder. Then you normally continue north, but I decided to get off the trail and wait for Tony in the shade of some trees. I ate a couple of carrots while I waited. At noon the shadows were quite dark under the trees and I knew she wouldn't spot me. Besides, the park was fairly crowded that time of day.

Many riders passed, primarily in couples. At ten past twelve, I spotted Tony. She was alone and she looked like she'd been born on a horse. Knees tight in, rear bouncing easily, hands firm on the bridle. The sleeves of her white shirt were rolled up above the elbows and her jodhpurs were full at the hips, tapered at the knees, fringed down the sides. Prince was sleek as hell, broad in the brisket, tremendous confirmation. He had a clean white streak from his forelock to his nostrils, and all four shanks were white all the way to the hooves, like neat white socks.

After she passed, I put the cycle in low gear and went after her. When I finally pulled alongside, she looked very surprised. I held my handlebars like a bridle, bounced up and down on my seat. That got a smile out of her. She slowed Prince to a gait, sort of a stop-and-go gait; I responded by doing a wheelie. She broke away in a gallop; I blasted after her, leaving a cloud of black cinders. She reined him to a sudden stop; I squealed to a stop, cinders spewing ahead. We eyed each other. She gave me a "try this" face, eased him into a difficult, ankle-crossing sideways step. I threw up my arms in defeat.

We both laughed softly. The ball was in her court, and she knew it. She was paying twenty-six dollars for two short hours, she obviously loved to ride, and she could easily have just said something polite and galloped away. Instead, she looked in my eyes, trotted Prince off the trail to a wide area of trees over near the reservoir and dismounted. I followed her slowly, got off nearby, kicked the stand, grabbed my saddlebags.

The next half hour was very strange. We didn't do a hell of a lot of talking. I fed the carrots to Prince, and he really loved them. We sat on the grass and drank the thermos of coffee from a single cup. We enjoyed the people wandering around. I remember a black kid riding a bike, wearing earphones, transistor radio stuck in his belt; he was sort of dancing with his bike as he rode along. A mother on roller skates was pushing a baby carriage; she was very, very pregnant. When I saw her, I glanced at Tony. She seemed to be digging that, too.

"Don't you just love nature?" I asked.

"You know it."

"Does this count as a real date?"

"No. No way. Has to be a movie, theater, dinner or dancing."

"I can do everything but dance."

"Unhappy childhood. Failure at the sock hop."

"You kidding? The war in Vietnam was nothing compared to my first sock hop. Took me an hour, but I finally worked up enough nerve to ask this girl, Eleanor Zoldoz, to dance. We start. In ten seconds, she stops. 'Why'd you ask me to dance if you didn't know how?' Well, I just died. Remember how we 'just died'? Went outside. It was raining. Walked around for an hour, cursing my life. When I got back, the dance was over. Gym was closed. My shoes were inside. Walked home in my socks in the rain. I get in the house. My dad roars from the bedroom: 'So, you're finally home! All you think about is having fun!' "

Tony laughed softly, glanced away as Prince started wandering over to us. Actually, he came over to me, looking for more carrots.

"Watch out," she told me. "He bites."

"Oh, yeah? You don't know who you're talking to." I leaned forward. "Come here, Prince."

When he came closer, I made the sound of a horse. Not the cliché whinnying sound, but a series of soft little neighs and lip blows. Prince gave me a look, lowered his head more. I spoke quietly into his ear, the kind of contented little sounds horses make in their stalls at night. When he answered me, I gave him a gentle scratch on the neck.

Tony shook her head in disbelief. "You certainly have a way with horses."

"Animals and kids adore me. That just leaves the rest of the world." I smiled at her then, an open smile.

I remember how she returned the smile almost seductively, the first time she even came close to doing that, and her question was just as unexpected. "You were in the building when Long was killed, weren't you?"

I glanced around. Just beyond the nearby trees, two girls were sunbathing. Three or four construction workers were eating sandwiches, watching the girls. Couples were sitting on blankets having lunch. The distant sound of traffic noises was punctuated by the relaxing sound of trotting hooves on cinders.

I kept my eyes averted. "Let's say I told you."

"Let's say you did."

"What happens then?"

"Never can tell. People, I hear, are brought closer together by the secrets they share."

"I just don't know why it's not enough that I'm crazy about you. I am, you know. I've watched you for over six months. I've seen more of you than my family. I really like you. Isn't that enough? Say yes."

"No. It would be if I could believe you."

"So how can I make you believe me?"

"By trusting me." She reached into the breast pocket of her shirt, took out a card, handed it to me. "Till then, my number."

"Would you like mine?"

She stood up. "I've got your number, Mr. Deever."

I looked at the card. It was engraved, with her name in a small, delicate typeface. "Antonia Sokolow. What's that, Russian?"

"Yes."

"So, you're the enemy."

She pursed her lips, reminding me of Linda. I got up, intending to help her mount, but she mounted quickly and easily without me. She paused, looking down at me.

"I'm not the enemy, Daryll."

"I know."

"I hope to hear from you."

"You will."

You sure will, I thought, as she trotted toward the track. And, standing there in the bright sun, watching her, I felt high again, really pleased with myself, with the way we were progressing. Okay, I'd forced it, but she didn't have to pick up on it, nobody was twisting her arm. And I knew she was using me, I understood the fact only too well. That was fine, for a start. She wanted something from me. I wanted something from her much, much more. She wanted something from me and she wasn't above utilizing everything at her disposal to get it. That game takes two players, the last I heard, and I understood the rules. And fear? Oh, God. At that moment, fear was as distant as death.

Less than six hours later, the opposite was true. I had a shock at work that night that frightened me badly and gave me the first clear indication of how complicated and dangerous the whole situation was to become. Looking back, the incident itself still seems unreal. I remember it only in flashes, like fragments from a dream, and I don't really want to think about it.

Mr. Long's son worked late that night. I'd finished almost all my work on the second floor and was emptying the trash baskets of the office next to Long's when I heard voices coming from his office. It sounded like his radio was on, a talk show or something. I slammed the door, as usual, pushed the trash wagon toward Long's office, expecting to hear his door open just before I got there. It didn't. The two trash baskets were already there on the floor, each half full. I emptied them quickly, glanced at the frosted glass as I replaced them. I saw his dark silhouette in fairly sharp contrast, as if he were standing close to the door. Then I heard the voices clearly. I stood there frozen and listened:

"You certainly have a way with horses."

"Animals and kids adore me. That just leaves the rest of the world."

"You were in the building when Long was killed, weren't you?"

"Let's say I told you."

"Let's say you did."

"What happens then?"

"Never can tell. People, I hear, are brought closer together by the secrets they share."

I remember backing away from that door, that silhouette, those voices. I looked down the empty corridor. It seemed to blur, pulsate, then start to move away from me. I began running. The hallway became progressively longer, walls, doors, floor, ceiling rushing away to a distant vanishing point. And I was moving slowly, laboriously, as if trying to run underwater. The next thing I remember with any degree of real clarity is being in the lobby, running toward the front door, getting out, and looking up at Long's lighted windows as I drove away.

I went straight home, made certain everything was locked, then tried to get my head together. I started with the most basic question: How could he have taped that conversation?

In the service, I'd learned just enough about electronic surveillance techniques to know that high-frequency "targeted" recording equipment had been used by intelligence agencies for years and could pick up conversations as far as three hundred feet away. My hunch was that Long had hired one or more of his associates to tail me with such a device every time I left the apartment. A man or woman, or both, could easily have been concealed behind any number of trees near us in the park, or they could've operated in the open. It could've been done by one of the couples having lunch nearby. I seemed to remember practically all of them had lunch boxes or baskets or bags of one kind or another. And a few of those couples were much closer than three hundred feet, probably half that distance. With today's technology, it wasn't that big a deal.

Next logical question: Why? Very few alternatives, as I saw it: Either Long had strong suspicions that I was the killer (or accomplice), or he had reason to believe that I'd witnessed the crime or at least seen the killer. Now, with the tape recording, he was probably certain he was on the right track and was trying to intimidate me. Or torture me. Or, very possibly, both. He'd succeeded that night.

Well, enough is enough. I finally decided to go to somebody for help. I got out Tony's card, dialed the number. Her voice answered on a recording device:

"Hello, this is Tony Sokolow. I'm out at the moment, but if you leave a message I'll get back to you as soon as possible. Please wait for the beep before talking. Thank you."

I waited, took a deep breath, tried to stay loose. "Hello, Tony. First things first: I miss you. Although my job as a janitor is very satisfying, somehow it's not enough. Let's get together. I'll tell you some things you want to know. I was there when it happened. Call me."

Next, I called George Fox, explained that I'd been sick at work and had to come home. It was one of the few nights I'd ever missed on the job, so he was nice about it, seemed very understanding. Said not to sweat it, that the day crew would take care of it. He also told me that he'd started interviewing for Aldo's replacement and that he'd try to have a new man within a week or so. So that was good news.

I watched television until about one o'clock, then began to feel very restless. I didn't feel like a regular meal, but I had a craving for fresh fruit. Ralph and I both liked fruit; his favorite was peaches. There was a good all-night delicatessen just around the corner, so I thought, what the hell. I was going to take Ralph with me, as usual, but I decided he'd be more valuable to me in the apartment. It was difficult, but I knew I had to start thinking that way.

Well, it was Thursday night, so Sheridan Square was pretty empty. The deli had only a couple of customers. I bought a dozen peaches, came back quickly, went in the vestibule, shifted the bag as I reached for my keys. A hand touched my right shoulder. I think I yelled as I spun around, and I remember peaches flying all over and a voice saying, "It's me, it's me." Jesus Christ, it was Linda. I was never so glad to see her face in my life, but I was also shaken up and angry.

"Why didn't you wait inside the apartment?"

She looked around at the peaches on the floor. "I lost the keys. I've been losing everything lately, my wallet, my umbrella. I must be going through something."

"What's up?"

"Maybe I missed you."

I started picking up the peaches. "What, you're not sure?"

She squatted down and helped, placing them carefully in the bag. She seemed very depressed. "I must be going through something. I'm not sure of anything. Maybe it's a phase, huh?"

I hadn't seen her or even talked with her since Monday out at my parents', and I was really glad she'd come over. I needed her that night, selfishly, but I think she needed me almost as much. When we got upstairs, she played with Ralph and didn't say very much, which was not that unusual, but I knew something was wrong, something serious. I just sensed it. I asked her to stay over, and she just nodded quickly, went in the bedroom and got undressed.

I brought in some peaches and we sat up in bed and talked.

"I just feel all nervous," she said finally. "Ever since our parents died, Aldo feels he has to look after me and make plans for me. Thinks I'm too young to look after myself. You have the key to my place?"

"Sure."

"Mine was in my wallet and I lost my wallet."

"I'll give you back your key. Calm down, huh?"

"If I could calm down I wouldn't be losing everything. I read that it's very Freudian when you lose stuff. Maybe it's a goddam Freudian phase I'm going through." She began crying. Very suddenly. "I don't know why. Shit, for all I know it could be something stupid like a vitamin deficiency." Then she blurted it out. "Aldo wasn't with me that night that guy got killed. I had to talk to these cops and I told them he was. But he wasn't."

I felt something grab in my stomach. "Where is he?"

She could hardly get the words out. "I don't know."

"Linda, look at me. Listen. I know how it seems to you, but just listen. Okay, he needed you to cover for him. He was probably by himself when the thing happened, he had no alibi, he was scared. That's perfectly normal. Let me tell you something about Aldo. He couldn't kill—*anybody*. Even in the war, he couldn't do it."

"He's got all this *money* all of a sudden. He says he won it at Harry's, but I—" She stopped crying as quickly as she'd started, and her voice dropped. "I hate to lie. I really hate to lie."

"Yeah, I know," I told her quietly. "I called and checked with Harry, too. Said he hadn't seen Aldo in two months."

13

TONY RETURNED MY CALL about three o'clock the next afternoon, and we agreed to meet as soon as I finished work. I selected a little Village restaurant called Karen Roy's, on Downing Street near Bedford, an area not frequented by tourists. It was a special place, informal and not too expensive, Oriental food and decor, and I knew the owner, Karen, an American who'd lived in Hong Kong for some years. It was our first real date, and I wanted it to be memorable. Also, I was anxious to show Tony off to Karen. I looked forward to that all day, and it kept me going at work that night. I'd called Aldo three or four times in the afternoon and hadn't caught him, so I kept trying at work during coffee breaks. Finally, I called Linda. She'd been trying to get him, too; several times she'd let it ring and ring, thinking he might be asleep. I told her to keep trying and that I'd check with her before midnight. When I did, she still hadn't reached him.

I quit work a little early, had a long shower, took my time getting ready. I shaved, brushed my teeth, even slapped on some aftershave. I mean, first date with Tony, you kidding? When I walked out of that building, I felt good, looked good, smelled good, best sports clothes, the whole shot. Only thing was, I was running a little late. The date was for one-thirty and it was ten past. To avoid the Friday-night crowds, particularly in the Village, I split over Forty-second to Seventh, took it straight down. Not too bad. Waiting for the light at Bedford, I glanced at my watch. Almost exactly one-thirty; I'd be a few minutes late at most. Took Bedford south past Leroy and Carmine, hung a right into Downing. As usual, no tourists in sight and almost no traffic.

I was a block away when I saw Tony in front of the restaurant. She was in trouble. Two men who looked Oriental were arguing with her, and a car had just pulled up to the curb near them. I was only half a block away when one of the men pulled a gun and the other took her arm and started walking her to the car. Within seconds, they were in the car, doors slamming as they pulled away. Instantly, the streetside back door swung open, Tony jumped out, tumbled and sprawled in the street, jumped up and ran toward my cycle. By that time I was going so fast I went right past her, hit the brakes, heard the rear tire burn and squeal, felt it fishtail side to side. I stuck my left foot out in the street, made a skidding sharp U-turn that almost spun me in a circle, straightened fast, blasted ahead, saw the two men jump out and sprint after Tony. I yanked off my helmet, slammed the slower guy in the back of the head, saw him fall, then hit the other man in the side of the face as he turned. He fell forward and I saw the gun bounce ahead in the street, throwing sparks. I lost my balance then, dropped my helmet, hit the brakes, skidded sideways, stopped. Tony rushed over, jumped on, grabbed my waist hard. I took off as fast as I could, but the car was already alongside on our right. He swerved sharply left, I jumped the curb, bounced back, kept going, felt for the little fire extinguisher below my seat. I yanked it out, took one quick glance at the driver before I pulled the trigger. Foam shot out with tremendous force, hit the car, splashed back on us. I didn't actually see it hit the driver, but it must have, because he lost control of the car almost immediately and began swerving crazily as we reached the corner, forcing me to jump the curb again. I drove along the sidewalk, skipped off the curb into Bedford and blasted away. Never found out what happened to the car.

We went directly to my apartment. Tony's hands, elbows and knees were scraped enough to draw blood, but the wounds weren't deep. She was badly shaken, and so was I. It took us a while to calm down. I used a washcloth to clean her up, then used cotton soaked in hydrogen peroxide solution on the scrapes. She was on the couch, and I remember how uncomfortable she seemed with all the attention, almost embarrassed, as if she wasn't used to being cared for. I enjoyed every minute of it. When it was all over, we talked about the incident. All she really knew was that they looked Vietnamese, they wanted some information out of her, and they meant business.

Later on, I went in the kitchen to make some instant coffee. When the water was boiling, I called out to her, "Hope you like it black. I don't have any milk."

She didn't answer.

I waited a few seconds, then: "Tony?"

No answer. I took the kettle off, turned off the gas, walked into the living room. She was gone. Ralph looked up at me, tilted his head to the side as he always did when he wasn't sure what was going on. I didn't know either. All I knew was that I felt suddenly very alone. I turned to go back in the kitchen when I heard her voice:

"Black is fine!"

She was in the bedroom. I went in there fast, with Ralph right behind me. Tony was sitting on the bed taking off her shoes. She looked over and smiled. I couldn't believe it.

"The luck of the Irish," I said softly.

She looked beautiful in the soft lamplight. "Let's make a deal. In the movies, people make love and then they give each other the third degree afterwards: 'How was it for you? Was it great? Was it wonderful? Was it, really?' Let's not do that afterwards."

"No, let's not. I'll tell you ahead of time. It's going to be wonderful." I looked at her for a while. "Coffee . . . before or after?"

"As long as it's not during."

Ralph trotted into the room, tail wagging, and looked up at me to see if everything was okay. I nodded that it was, pointed for him to leave. He did, and I closed the door after him.

About an hour later, we had our coffee in bed. We sat there and talked quietly in the dim light, and I loved everything about her. It was a strangely relaxed conversation, as if we'd known each other for years. Ordinarily, I never talked to anyone about the war, but when she asked questions about it, I didn't mind answering. I answered as honestly as I knew how.

"Vietnam was full of reporters," I told her. "There we were, killing and dying, and this army of reporters was looking for a story."

"It was their job. Were you drafted?"

"No, I volunteered."

"Why?"

"It was my job. That's how I saw it. I try to do what seems to be the right thing at the time. That way I have no regrets. What do you do when you're not doing stories?"

"Oh, I make up stuff. I'll interview a fat lady with a bunch of kids, a lottery winner. And I'll go home and think how nice it would be to be fat and sloppy and have a bunch of kids who adore me. Then I'll do a story about somebody who devotes his whole life to helping others, and I wonder what it'd be like to have a calling, a cause. Back and forth."

"The rich daydream too? You *are* rich, aren't you?"

"Very." She said it matter-of-factly.

"The rich always marry the rich. Why is that?"

"It's the only people they know."

"But what if this rich lady met this real nice guy? I mean, he's not poor, but—what happens then?"

"Then the rich lady would have to decide."

"Why's it always the rich that decide?"

"You're the one who's deciding, Daryll. We met tonight because you had something to tell me."

I took a long look in her eyes. "I'll tell you everything in the morning. But I'm warning you. Once I do, you won't have any more excuses for seeing me. It'll have to be because you want to."

She nodded, held my gaze. "Or don't want to."

When I woke up in the morning, Tony wasn't in bed. The room was in soft sunlight, and Ralph was sitting on the floor looking up at me. She had to be in the bathroom or the kitchen. I reached for my glasses on the nightstand, put them on, glanced instantly at the chair where she'd laid her clothes. It was empty. No. No, she must be in the kitchen making us some breakfast. I jumped out of bed, put on my jeans fast, then walked, didn't run, to the kitchen. It was dark and empty. Grabbed my keys, ran to the front door, stumbled over Ralph, stopped, ran back to check the bathroom. Empty. Bolted for the door again, down the stairs, tripping on Ralph, through the vestibule, out in the street. No sign of her in either direction. Ralph was barking. I was fighting for breath. "Son of a bitch," I said. "Knew it was too good. Knew it. Knew it."

We went back up slowly. The apartment seemed empty and depressing. I remember sitting on the couch and lighting a cigarette. Well, there was one good thing. She'd left without trying to get the information she wanted. That was intriguing. I wondered if it meant what I wanted it to mean.

I think I sat on that couch most of the morning, smoking, drinking coffee, thinking about her. I loved that girl so much I didn't care about anything else. It had never happened to me before, and I just didn't know how to handle it. I simply couldn't get enough of her. Last night I'd done stuff like stare at her openly, and I was happy just to touch her and listen to her voice and be with her. I couldn't believe it was over. I just couldn't accept that. Because, if it was true, if it was over, where the hell would I go from there? What would I do then? Go back to watching her on the news? No way. Well, yes, if it came to that, yes. It was better than nothing. I couldn't possibly just cut her out of my life. Not yet, at least. It would be much too painful. And, after last night, I couldn't go back to Linda again. That was out of the question. I'd have to explain it to Linda. I'd have to tell her flat out.

I half expected Tony to call me that afternoon, to say something, anything. Instead, I got a call from Aldo. Said he had to see me right away. Said he had fantastic news. Well, I wasn't really up to dealing with the guy at that point, but I told him to come over. When I asked him where he'd been all day yesterday, he said it was part of his news, that he'd explain everything when he saw me.

He arrived about twenty minutes later and he was all business. Took a fat envelope out of his pocket, pulled out business forms, profit-and-loss statements, legal forms, spread them out on the coffee table.

"I found a place," he told me. "Broadway near Ninety-seventh. Two old guys and they're retiring and we get to keep the stock. They got everything, they got stock you wouldn't believe. Nice location and a real sweet deal."

"How much?"

"They said they'll carry us. That means we make a down payment and then pay them in monthly installments. Only eight percent interest. That's good, you know? Eight percent."

"How much is the down payment?"

"Fifty grand."

"And you got fifty grand?"

"Yeah. I told you, I won big."

"I talked to Harry, Aldo."

"Yeah, well, you know Harry, he never—"

"He says he hasn't seen you in ages."

Aldo laughed, straightened his papers. "You know Harry, he lies. Whenever that kind of bread's involved, he covers himself. Hey, I told Linda about the store this morning. She's absolutely thrilled. Once we get in the store, once we start making it, you two could get engaged. You realize that?"

"She's awfully young, Aldo."

"What's that supposed to mean? Young's good, man. Everybody wants them young. What're you talking about?"

"Linda and I are breaking up, but that's not the point. The point is, you're in a lot of trouble."

"Don't tell *me* what the point is! Who you got? You got somebody else, is that it? I'm asking you, man, is that it?"

I decided to test his reaction. "I was there when Long was killed, Aldo. I saw you."

He picked up the papers, began stuffing them back in the envelope. "You goddam traitor. You led Linda on all this time. You led *me* on all this—"

"You're not keeping your eye on the ball, Aldo. You're in a lot of trouble."

"I know that. You think I don't know that? Who you got, huh? It's that TV woman, right? That who you got, the TV woman?"

I stood up, stepped away. The guy was really working himself into a state. I'd only seen him that way a couple of times before, both during combat. Instead of concentrating on the job to be done, he'd lash out at something else, anything that could distract his attention.

He jammed the envelope in his pocket, stood up fast, walked toward me. "You think she likes *you?* That what you think? She's just using you! You're a *janitor,* you asshole! You think a woman like that . . . ? You can't be *trusted,* man!"

He took one step toward the door, then threw a punch from nowhere and caught me hard on the cheek. In an almost automatic reflex, I threw a right hand that slammed into his nose. Blood spurted out immediately, and Aldo seemed to go crazy then. He screamed, jumped at me, and I saw Ralph scramble in from the kitchen as we both hit the floor. Ralph leaped on Aldo, growling viciously, but not biting. Aldo grabbed my neck and squeezed with everything he had. On my back, struggling to breathe, unable to tell Ralph it was for real, I remember the sudden realization that I was fighting for my life. I slammed my knee into his groin. He jumped back fast, yelling with the pain, holding himself, spinning away from Ralph.

I got up fast, holding my throat, coughing, trying to get air. Ralph stopped as soon as he saw me stand. I leaned back against the wall. My voice was hoarse and shaking. "Goddam you, Aldo. Did you really kill Long?"

He pulled himself up by the arm of the couch, started for the door. "Didn't think I could do it, did you? Now you've got the story to tell your girlfriend."

He was still crouched and holding himself when he left. As soon as the door slammed, Ralph looked at me, and I think he sensed for the first time that it hadn't been a game. I continued to lean against the wall and feel my throat. Ralph's ears went back, he lowered his head, walked over to me, crying then, stood on his hind legs, placed one paw on my stomach and began patting me with the other. I stroked his head, told him it was okay.

It was warm and my windows were open. I heard a certain sound from the street that I instantly distinguished from all other traffic noises: the blast of a motorcycle starting directly below. My brain told me it couldn't possibly be mine, it was locked, but my instincts took me to the windows, quickly. I was on the second floor, so there was no mistake: Aldo was pulling away on my cycle.

God, that really infuriated me. I watched him snake down West Fourth, hang a left at O'Henry's and disappear into the traffic on Sixth. I ran into the kitchen. My cycle keys and door keys were still on the counter where I always left them. How in hell could he have done it? Where was he going? Not to his apartment. To Linda's?

Then I remembered: Linda was working that Saturday, she'd told me that. The theatrical wardrobe shop where she was a cutter was doing a double-time crash project that weekend for the Monday-night opening of an off-Broadway black musical of some kind. She'd be at work all day. Knowing Aldo, he'd head there first before he did anything crazy.

I grabbed my keys, went in the bedroom for my wallet. The telephone rang. It was my mother, crying. When I got her calmed down enough to make sense, she told me she'd had a terrible argument with my father. He'd left the house. He'd wheeled himself out on the sidewalk of Astoria Boulevard, and that was the last she'd seen of him. She'd called the bar where he hung out, she'd called two of his drinking buddies, she'd even called his bookie. Nobody had seen him.

"What time did he leave?" I asked.

"Right after breakfast, at least three hours ago."

"You think he's headed here?"

"Daryll, he would've grabbed a cab, you know that. He would've been there in half an hour."

"He's probably out on a toot, Mother. That's all I can think of. He picked some bar you wouldn't know. What was the argument about?"

She didn't answer.

"Mother? What was it about?"

She was crying softly. "He said he's leaving me. He said it's over. He said it's been over for six years."

I took the uptown express to Times Square, walked quickly up Broadway to Forty-third. The front of Linda's shop was crowded with black actors and actresses being fitted for African-style outfits. I rushed past them, past hundreds of costumes hanging from racks and pipes, past dozens of half-dressed dummies, and into the back room. It was very hot, crowded with women cutting and sewing at long tables. Linda was cutting fabric and looked exhausted, hair pulled back and tied with a rubber band, face sweating, pins in her mouth. When she saw me rush in the door, she spit out the pins fast.

"Don't do that to me," she said. "That's the second time today. Aldo burst in here like a madman."

"Know where he is now?"

"He burst in, he burst out."

"Didn't say where he was going?"

"He never says where he's going."

"He got any friends I don't know about?"

"You're it. He thinks you're the best thing that ever—"

"All right, all right. Why'd he come here? What'd he want?"

She frowned, stood up, grabbed the fabric she was cutting and walked over to a dummy. "He asked me stuff."

"What kind of stuff?"

"Stuff. You know." She fitted the fabric around the dummy's torso, started pinning it.

"Stuff the stuff, Linda. Tell me. It's important."

"I know, I know. But it's hard, you know?"

"I don't know a thing. You're telling me nothing. 'You know, you know.' "

She pressed in the last pin, wiped her forehead. "He—you know, he wanted to know the same old stuff: 'Hey, Linda, you crazy about him, right? I'm asking you.' He wanted to know if I loved you." She was close to tears then. "So I told him. I said—I said no. Then he got all weird. Started ranting and all. Said it was all my fault." She looked up at me, trying to find the words. "I had to say no. I've got to start being an honest person, Daryll." Finally, she was crying. "We can't get engaged. I can't marry you. I can't."

"Hey, don't cry. It's all right. I can't marry you either."

She was crying and didn't hear. "I'm sorry. You're so nice. Aldo had all these plans, you know? But, I don't know. I just don't love you."

I touched her face. "That's all right. I don't love you either."

"You're just saying that to make me feel better."

"No, I swear. I really don't love you."

She seemed to cheer up a little. "Is that really true?"

I nodded, spoke softly. "I never loved you."

She looked almost happy. "I never loved you either."

"So, you see?"

"Oh, thank God. We don't have to be crazy about each other any more." She put her arms around me quickly, hugged me, kissed me on the cheek.

"I got to go, Linda. If you see or hear from Aldo, tell him to stay put. And call me. You hear?"

"Is he in a lot of trouble?"

"Yes. Over his head."

14

I've always loved to read, and one of my favorite novels is *The Way of All Flesh,* by Samuel Butler. It was his last book, and by far his best and most famous. At least, in my opinion. When he died in 1902 at the age of sixty-seven, he'd recently completed the novel, but it wasn't published until the following year. I've often wondered if Butler actually saw the book in print. Probably not, but at least he had the satisfaction of finishing it and realizing what he'd accomplished. Sometimes I go back and reread certain passages of that book, and one that always haunted me, and always will, is found in Chapter 14: "Every man's work, whether it be literature or music or pictures or architecture or anything else, is always a portrait of himself." When I read that sentence for the first time about ten years ago, I don't think I really understood it, but I do now. I think it's a true statement, and that's what continues to haunt me. I don't like the portrait of myself. I don't like the reality of it. It's one of the things that makes me bleed. I don't want to die before I do something, anything, to radically change that portrait. But I have a terrible, gnawing fear that it's already too late, that I've wasted a gift I was given, that I'll die with the agony of that knowledge.

Monday night at work, I came close to death, and I experienced precisely that feeling. It was at the end of my shift and I was alone in the basement dumping one of the last loads into the trash compactor. As I did, I heard the sound of bottles clinking against each other. All tenants are reminded periodically not to put bottles in their wastebaskets. Bottles have been known to explode under the pressure of the compacting process, which can screw up the machine; but, more important, when some poor slob like me opens the front door of the machine after the process, he can get hit by flying glass.

Anyway, when I heard the bottles clinking, I was pissed off, of course, because I should've caught them earlier when I dumped the baskets. I was very tired now, and it just meant extra work. Not that it was the first time it'd happened by any means. I suppose, on the average, bottles would make it all the way to the compactor stage maybe once or twice a month. Once they're in the machine, you have absolutely no alternative but to climb in the damn thing, scrounge around the top layer of trash till you find them, and take them out by hand.

Well, as I said, I'd been dumping one of the last loads, so the machine was fairly full. I climbed down into the machine, using the little steel ladder. I'd found four of the bottles when I heard a noise in the basement. I froze, holding the bottles, listening. After a few seconds, I heard it again. A footstep? I waited. Another sound. Leather on cement. No question. Soft. Slow. Now another. Soft. Slow. Another. Approaching the machine. I didn't move. I knew if I took even a deep breath, the bottles would clink. I looked around at the steel walls, half in shadow, angular shadows. The footsteps stopped. Silence. Then they started again and sounded very close to the machine. They stopped. Whoever was out there was standing right next to the front of the machine. I felt sweat drip down my face. I looked up at the light bulbs in the basement ceiling. Would he turn them off? Total silence. It seemed to last a long time. Then I heard a sudden, sharp sound—*Click!*—followed immediately by the earsplitting roar and screech of the huge steel compactor lid moving toward me. Instantly, involuntarily, I was crouching and holding my ears, and whatever chance I had of scrambling up the ladder was gone. Light from the ceiling was quickly being obscured. I was shaking and screaming, but I couldn't hear my voice in the deafening thunder of the lid. Then the last sliver of light was eclipsed. Total darkness. Blood rushed to my head, I lost all control, ran around blindly, slammed into the walls, bounced off, screamed at the top of my lungs. I seem to remember smelling the filth on the steel lid before it touched my head, softly, then the palms of my hands were against it. It felt slimy, cold, damp. The stench became overpowering. I dropped to my knees in the trash. I stopped screaming. Abruptly. I started crying then, really crying, knowing I had only seconds left, and tried to think of a prayer, any prayer. Vomit filled my mouth and gushed out and my mind went blank.

The next thing I remember was the distant sound of an alarm ringing, like a fire alarm. The noise of the compactor stopped. The alarm kept ringing, far away in the dark. I knew what it was. He'd pushed the emergency stop button. Crying, covered in vomit, I remained on my knees, reached up and touched the lid. It seemed to be about a foot over my head then. And I remember thinking: Why torture me like this? Why make me suffer like this? Finish it! The alarm stopped. Silence. Five seconds. Ten. *Click!* The machine exploded into sound again. I fell back on the trash, holding myself, shivering in the heat and smell. Then I realized the sound was different. Just as loud, but more high-pitched. The retraction gear. I waited in the dark, listening, then scrambled to my feet, reached up, touched the lid. It was moving up, slowly, laboriously, reeking with stench. In fifteen, twenty seconds, I saw a crack of light. It widened slowly. I was already stumbling to the side ladder, reaching, grabbing, clawing at the tiny steel rungs. I was at the top before the space was large enough for me to squeeze through, hands over the edge, waiting, out of breath, heart pounding, not caring who was out there, not caring about anything in the world but getting out.

Then I was on the loading platform on my hands and knees. I looked down and saw Aldo. Neither of us said a word for a long time. Finally, painfully, I got up, steadied myself on the railing, walked down the steps one at a time. He was staring at the machine fixedly.

"What the hell you doing in there?" he asked.

I coughed, tested my voice. "Why didn't you finish it?"

"Jesus. It was habit." He turned, looked at me. "I saw the top open and I pressed the button. It was habit. You okay?"

"Why didn't you finish it, Aldo?"

He ignored that, glanced around. "Thought I'd hide out here. Nobody'd think of looking for me here. Shit, Daryll, nothing's working out. I wanted you two to get married. I wanted—like a family. A place to go on Thanksgiving and Christmas. You know. I open the door: Hey, here's Aldo. Everybody glad to see me."

"You don't kill a man for that."

He looked away, shook his head. "I didn't kill him."

I wanted to believe him, but I couldn't. "Come on, Aldo. It's too late for that."

"I appreciate your thinking I did. But I couldn't."

"Yeah. So where'd you get the money?"

"Loan sharks. Twenty-five grand from these Italian guys in New Jersey, twenty-five grand from some Italian guys in Brooklyn. Now they're after me."

I hesitated. "Then why the hell'd you let me think—?"

"I don't know. I was—I was always such a coward. You know that. Everybody in our outfit knew it, but it was you knowing it that hurt. It still hurts. I wish I'd killed that bastard. So help me, Daryll, I wish I had."

"These loan sharks. You can give them back the money."

He shook his head slowly. "I bought the store."

I just looked at him for a while. Then I walked to the locker room. He followed in silence. I threw my uniform in the laundry hamper, took a long shower and tried to calm down. But the longer I thought of what he'd done to me in there the angrier I got. I felt angry, weak and sick when I came out. Aldo sat on the bench and watched me get dressed. He looked very depressed. He should've been. I was tired of his lies, his whole routine. I'd had it with him.

"Aldo, you realize you almost killed me in there?"

"I swear to God, I didn't know you were in there."

"Bullshit. You got a *screw* loose, man. You know that? You're *sick*. You need help."

"I know I do."

"Then *do* something about it!"

"I *can't* right now! You *know* that!"

"I knew you were a sick man the first time I ever met you!"

"Oh, thanks. Thanks for that."

"You tried to *choke* me Saturday! Right or wrong?"

"Wrong! I was just—I was just so pissed off I couldn't *think!"*

"Then you tried to kill me *tonight!* Except you chickened out!"

"No!" He stood up, turned away, shoved his hands in his pockets.

"If you weren't such a *chicken,* you could be a real killer!"

"Daryll. Daryll, don't do this."

"Admit it! Face *up* to it! You're a *psycho,* man!"

He kept his back turned, spoke so softly I could hardly hear. "Okay. All right. I'm a psycho. I'm a sick man. I'm also a coward. You knew that when you met me, and I knew it. But you accepted me as your friend. And I needed a friend, believe me. And so did you. And we went through a lot together, you and me. And now that's all ancient history and everybody says to forget it. Except what we saw we can't ever forget. Ever. I came back worse than I went in. We both know that. I came out hurt, Daryll. I did, let's face the fact. I got hurt bad. Real bad, and it can't be fixed. You're the only guy who knows that. Being friends, doesn't that mean understanding when nobody else understands?"

I went over to the mirror and combed my hair. "Stay here tonight. And stay put. You got a key, right?"

"Right."

I watched him in the mirror. "How'd you get my cycle started?"

He shrugged. "Piece of cake. Jimmied the wheel lock, jumped the engine. Used the jumper wire from your trunk."

"Jimmied the trunk?"

"Child's play."

"Where's it parked?"

"Usual place out front."

"Locked?"

He looked offended. "Hey. Huh? I may be bananas, but I ain't stupid."

"For Christ's sake, get out of here before the day crew arrives. Call me in the afternoon. Don't wake me up."

As I started toward the door, he grabbed my arm and looked in my eyes. "Thanks, Daryll."

Well, I swear to God, when I went upstairs and walked through the lobby, I wasn't at all convinced that he was innocent. First, you have to understand one important thing about the guy. In my judgment, Aldo was on the borderline of being a congenital liar. Over the years, I'd seen him in situations when I was quite certain he was incapable of distinguishing truth from fiction. He'd lie about something small, then have to cover that lie with another. And so on, the whole nine yards. Sometimes it just seemed to snowball on him, gradually, until the initial lie or series of lies finally buttressed a whole superstructure that he positively accepted as the truth of what actually happened. I mean, he'd swear on his life that it was the truth. And it wasn't. The whole thing was a lie. Years ago, I thought it was funny. So did he, in his way. But it wasn't funny. It was anything but funny, and I should've understood that and tried to help him. God, I really should've tried. I was his best friend and I stood around and laughed. I didn't know that it would get progressively worse. I really didn't have the slightest idea of how damaging it could be to him. I failed him that way, and I've regretted it deeply ever since.

I locked the front door, started down the steps toward my cycle, stopped suddenly. In the light from the streetlamp, I saw a slender, dark-haired woman in a white pantsuit standing next to my cycle, smoking, glancing at her watch. My eyes aren't that good, and I absolutely refused to believe it was Tony until I got closer. Then I *ran*. Ran down those steps and across the sidewalk and slowed at the last minute so I could put my arms around her gently and just hold her.

Just as gently, she maneuvered me to arm's length. "I didn't come here for that, Daryll."

I adjusted my glasses, smiled. "This looks like one of those 'there's another guy' scenes."

"It is. There is."

"And is he tall, handsome and rich?"

"Very, very and very."

"Then you have nothing to worry about. This is America. A guy like that can't possibly lose. But if he does, it must mean I've got something too. Come on. Let's go somewhere."

She considered it. "All right. I want you to come to my parents' place."

"It's kind of late."

"They're not home."

"All right. Where to?"

"Seventy-ninth and West End."

Her parents lived in one of the oldest and most distinguished apartment buildings in Manhattan, the Apthorp, 390 West End Avenue, on the southwest corner of Seventy-ninth. The building had been designated as an "Individual Historical Landmark" by the Landmarks Preservation Commission, which meant that the exterior couldn't be altered in any way. I don't know what the style of architecture was, but you entered through massive iron gates on the Broadway side of the building into a huge open courtyard with a circular cobblestone drive obviously designed for horse-drawn carriages. I parked the cycle there and we went into the apartment complex on the south side of the courtyard. A smartly uniformed elevator operator with white gloves greeted Tony warmly and took us to the sixth floor. There were only two apartments per floor. The spacious foyer had a spotless inlaid marble floor, mirrored walls and a very high ceiling.

Their apartment was just positively gigantic. That's the only word. I mean, it went on and on, quietly. If it's true that new money is loud and old money is quiet, then the Sokolow family must surely have been among the landed aristocracy in Russia for many generations. Now, I don't know all that much about old stuff, but even I could pick out a few things in the living room that you don't see in just ordinary digs: Aubusson carpets, gold and enamel Fabergé knickknacks on the mantel, a Coromandel screen in the corner, a Steinway grand piano. Oil paintings? Name an artist. Mirrors, chandeliers, grandfather clocks. In honesty, I was just a little afraid to touch things. Including Tony. I think she sensed this, because she went out of her way to make me relax. For example, she sat down at the piano and played me her favorite little tune, Mendelssohn's Trio No. 2 in C Minor; she explained that her mother accompanied her on cello and her father on violin. Somehow, it didn't seem to relax me a hell of a lot.

Finally, she brewed up some tea and stuck on Rachmaninoff's Concerto No. 2 in C Minor, Opus 18, and we had a long talk. I told her the whole story about discovering Long's body and being scared and running. It was the first time I'd told anybody except my father. And I remember what a relief it was.

"When I first saw you," I told her, "I just had to see you again. So I made it seem like I knew more than I did. It's that simple. That's the truth."

"It really doesn't matter anymore. I've quit my job."

"You—what?"

"I quit my job with Metro this afternoon."

"Why?"

"Oh, it's—complicated. I've been thinking about quitting for a long time now. I'm sick of subbing for people on a minute's notice. I'm tired of waiting in line for the regular drama critic's slot. I could wait years and years for that. I felt I was wasting time there. I could be doing other things, things I enjoy much more."

"So that's the end of the Long story. Even if I knew something, you wouldn't need it."

"I don't *need* anything, Daryll."

"I know. You mentioned things you enjoy more. What?"

"Maybe I'll devote myself to my music for a while."

I nodded, looked at her hands. "You've got sidelines that people make careers out of."

"That's the problem. One of them, anyway. As far back as I can remember, I was always doing things my parents wanted me to do. I took piano lessons from the age of five. *Five!* I was dragged along to concerts and recitals and benefits since I was old enough to *walk*. I was taught to speak Russian since I was old enough to *talk*. And ever since I was a little girl, my mother had this uncanny ability of telling me to do something that I was going to do myself. The very things I wanted to do for her out of love, she turned into commands. It's strange. I remember one day when we were in Paris. I was ten. I was in the park with my parents and I got lost. It felt wonderful to be lost. I started running. My heart was pounding. I began crying. I had no idea where I was, but it seemed very important to be alive, to stay alive. I stumbled out of the trees into a clearing and saw my parents. I wanted to tell them how strange and wonderful I'd felt, but they were angry at me for being late. We were going to miss the concert. They took my hands and walked me away, and I looked back over my shoulder as if I'd left my dearest friend in the forest, never to see her again. And I was right."

"I can see her." I stood up, went to her. "Let's get out of here, Tony. I hate tea. Let's get lost. Before somebody finds us."

15

YOU SHOULD DRIVE DOWN BROADWAY about two-thirty on a weekday morning. It's like having the city all to yourself. No traffic to speak of, not even the street cleaners or garbage trucks are out that early, no pedestrians to worry about, no polluted air, only a handful of police cars wandering around to keep you honest. On a cycle, it's nothing less than exhilarating, especially with someone you love. We had stretches of green lights for ten or twelve blocks at a clip, clear down to Columbus Circle where the divider ends, then we saw some semblance of nightlife around Times Square, where we picked up Seventh Avenue. From that point on, it was all our own, potholes and all, things that go bump in the night, all the way down to Sheridan Square. Seventy-five blocks in twenty-two minutes flat. Almost three and a half blocks a minute. Time it during rush hour some day.

When I unlocked my apartment door and snapped on the lights, I kept Tony behind me until I called out, "Not tonight, Ralph." He didn't show. I glanced around carefully, then waved Tony inside.

"I guess he's still shy of you."

When she came in and I closed the door and locked it, I continued to glance around. I didn't want him leaping out suddenly with her there.

"What's the matter?" she asked.

"I don't know. If he's not hiding, he's probably in the kitchen. He likes it best on the linoleum, you know? Sit down. Got a surprise for you."

"Love surprises."

I went to the video recorder, removed the tape, picked another from the shelf under the stand. "After I make coffee, I want you to see something with me. My favorite tape." I plugged it in.

"Give me a hint?"

"No hint."

"Fred Astaire and Ginger Rogers!"

"Nope."

"John Travolta and—Gene Kelly?"

"Even better. Be right back."

I went in the kitchen. Ralph wasn't there. I started for the bedroom, decided to put the kettle on first. I filled it, put it on the stove, turned on the gas, and was about to reach for the instant coffee when I heard Ralph growl from the living room. I went in there fast. He had been hiding behind the long window drapes, and now only his head appeared from the bottom. His eyes looked strange, and the corners of his mouth were white with traces of foam. Tony had already moved to the other side of the room. She looked very frightened. When you know animals as well as I do, and see foam at the corners of the mouth, you react on instinct rather than intellect, because you know how serious it is. I squatted down immediately, held my hands into my thighs, kept my voice low and calm:

"It's all right, Ralph. It's all right."

He growled, started moving toward me slowly in a crouch.

"Daryll, something's wrong with him."

I kept my eyes on him as I spoke to her: "Stay where you are. Don't move and don't speak. That's right, Ralph, come over here, let me take a look at you."

He continued advancing at me, low, growling from way down in his throat, a sound he'd never made before. His eyes were very wide and the pupils were dilated.

"Ralph's going to be all right, aren't you, Ralph? Nice and easy, Ralph. Come on, let me take a look at you."

As he came closer, he began snarling, lifting his upper lip, baring his teeth, and his hindquarters started moving rhythmically as they always did when he was ready to attack.

I gave him a firm command: "No! No, Ralph! No! You hear me! No, Ralph! No!"

His hindquarters slowed, he stopped snarling for a few seconds, and he glanced away from me, as if trying to remember something important.

"Sit! Sit, Ralph! Sit down there!"

He leaped at me so fast I didn't have time to move a muscle, hit me with his full weight, knocked me backward on the floor, snarling like crazy, snapping. I heard Tony scream, felt Ralph's teeth dig into my left arm. He held it between his jaws, shook his head frantically, tearing, mauling. I screamed, grabbed his throat with the other hand, squeezed, pushed with everything I had, began kicking wildly. He lunged for my throat, snapped at it, turned his head, snapped again and barely missed. I got my other hand on his throat, straightened both elbows, hung on, tried to roll him over, couldn't.

"Tony! The drawer by the *lamp! Gun! Gun!* Drawer by the *lamp! Fast!"*

I heard her run to the table, pull out the drawer, fumble through it. I had Ralph by the throat, but he kept lunging at my neck again and again, snapping, turning his head, snarling, snapping, and I knew I couldn't hold him back. Then I saw Tony behind him, holding my revolver but pointing it away from us, terrified, yelling something I couldn't hear.

"Get *close! Shoot!* Try not to hit me and *shoot!"*

"I *can't!"*

"Do it! Shoot!"

As she moved closer, holding the gun with both hands, Ralph swung his head back at her, fast, then went for my neck, then swung his head back at her again. I was losing my grip on his throat. On her knees, Tony pushed the gun deep into his chest and pulled the trigger. The blast was muffled, but the impact knocked him off me and into two very fast rolls. He landed on his side, facing us, and I remember his short, breathless little cries and the way his legs kept moving, as if trying to run away.

Tony put the gun on the floor and turned away. She was shaking and crying. I looked around for my glasses, found them, put them on. I picked up the gun, moved to Ralph on my knees. His eyes were wide open, looking at me. His jaw was slack and his tongue was out. He kept making the short little cries and trying to breathe. His legs had slowed and only his paws were moving. I placed the barrel softly against his chest, above the blood on his fur, up high where I'd so often felt his heart beating. My right hand was shaking so badly I had to steady it with the other. I was crying and I couldn't see. Everything was a blur. I pulled the trigger and felt his body jump. The cries stopped. I sat back on my ankles and put the gun down. I took off my glasses, wiped my eyes, put them back on. His paws seemed to tremble a little, stop, start again, then they were still. I became aware of a shrill, high-pitched whistling sound, building, getting higher. I didn't know what it was until Tony got up, went into the kitchen and took the kettle off. While she was out there, I moved over on my knees, picked Ralph up, sat back, cradled him on my lap, in my arms, and hugged him. I'd had him since he was a puppy. I'd had him since he was eight weeks old. I'd loved him more than I'd loved anything or anybody in my life. I gave him one last hug, kissed him, and said goodbye.

After I carried him into the bedroom and wrapped him in a blanket, I didn't know what to do. Tony came in and stood next to me for a while. Finally, we went back in the living room and sat down and she went to work on my left forearm. She'd gone through the medicine cabinet and had everything laid out on the table—hydrogen peroxide, alcohol, cotton, sterile pads, a roll of gauze, surgical tape, even scissors. Strangely, the wounds didn't seem to throb badly until she cleaned the blood away and I took a good look at them. Ralph's teeth marks were all the way around, relatively deep, some torn, but not enough to require stitches; at least, I didn't think so. As soon as Tony poured on the alcohol, the whole thing started burning like hell.

"You've got to see a doctor," she told me.

"I know."

"You could have a bad infection."

"We'll go to Bellevue Emergency."

"Could he have had rabies?"

"No. No, I took him for his walk this afternoon, he was perfectly okay. He hasn't been in contact with any other dogs, cats, any animals at all."

"Okay, all I'm saying, he had all the symptoms of rabies, as I understand them."

"Soon's you finish, we'll get over to Bellevue."

"Can you drive?"

"Sure. I'll be all right."

After swabbing on the hydrogen peroxide, which I knew wasn't anywhere near strong enough, she taped on the sterile pads. She was rolling the gauze around my arm when I focused on some kind of red substance on the floor near the drapes. I waited until she'd cut the gauze and taped it before going over to see. It was a small amount of what looked like hamburger. I picked it up, felt it, smelled it. It was wet, saturated with something odorless.

"What is it?" Tony asked.

"Somebody fed him some junk."

"What kind of junk?"

"I don't know. A drug of some kind, an odorless drug, probably tasteless. Not poison. Something that made him crazy. Crazy enough to want to kill me. How the hell did they get it *in* here?"

I stood up fast, went to the door, squatted down, felt the carpet right in front of the opening. Not only was it still damp, there were tiny bits of hamburger around.

"Somebody jimmied the lock," I said. "Opened the door just a crack, dumped the meat in, closed it quickly. The door locks automatically when you shut it."

"Why would anybody—"

"Whoever did this killed Long. And he'll be back."

She nodded. "Let's get the hell out of here. Right now."

As I stood, I remember experiencing a very strange sensation. I don't know if it was delayed shock or what, but I felt an overpowering sense of outrage and anger. I wanted to get my hands on the guy who did this and kill him. Nothing else would do. I wanted to point a gun at his face and blow his brains out. I wanted him to see me do it.

"Tony, I want you to get out of here. Go. Now."

"Are you *kidding?* Daryll, he's coming *back* here! For Christ's sake, don't try to be a *hero!* Let the *cops* be heroes, that's what they're paid for! You don't know what kind of a *madman* you're dealing with!"

I walked over to where I'd placed the gun, picked it up, looked at my watch. "If you're going, you better do it now."

She went to the table, started picking up the bandages and stuff. "We better have that coffee now. Could be a late night."

We were sitting on the couch, finishing the coffee in silence, when I heard it. I put my cup down, leaned forward. It's not that my ears are especially sharp, it's just that at that time of morning you don't need bionic hearing if you're paying attention. Tony frowned, put her cup down, listened, heard it too. Footsteps coming up the stairway, very, very slowly. We both stood up quietly. I motioned for her to go in the kitchen. She did. I picked up the gun, went to the door and turned off the lights. Then I gestured for her to hit the kitchen lights. When our eyes adjusted, we could see each other in the dim light from the windows. The footsteps continued slowly. I stood behind the door.

The footsteps stopped. I realized he was standing against the door listening, but I didn't expect him to knock. When he did, it startled me. He waited, knocked again, louder. I was breathing very quickly, too quickly. I took a deep breath and held it. He inserted something into the lock, worked it around slowly. Within seconds there was a relatively loud click in the tumbler and the latch snapped back. The door opened very slowly and a slender ribbon of yellow light from the hall expanded into a V. No shadow. He was standing back against the door, pushing it open by inches. Finally, his shadow appeared from the side of the V, moved into the middle, hesitated, then moved forward. I waited until he was almost all the way in before I stuck the gun into his lower back.

"One move and I shoot!"

He froze, hands by his sides, kicked the door into me and I pulled the trigger. *Click!* Empty! In the next split second, he pivoted in a crouch, slammed a fist into my stomach, knocked my breath out. I doubled over, lost the gun, and he was all over me, throwing punches so fast I couldn't see where they were coming from. I remember trying desperately to get my breath back, seeing colored sparks as I was hit, tumbling over a chair, landing on my back, scrambling up and running. He grabbed my shirt, spun me around, hit me with a left-right combination that sent me sprawling back into the TV set. The next thing I knew, I was on my stomach and he had a wire around my neck. I reached up with both hands, managed to get the fingers of my left hand under it before he yanked it tight. A quick image of Long's face flashed into my mind, the dark-blue color, the eyes wide, his fingers under the wire. I began kicking, thrashing, struggling with a frenzy I never thought possible as he tightened the wire. My right hand reached around wildly, trying to grab anything to use as a weapon, when I felt the TV set on the floor, screen facing up. I reached under it, felt the video recorder controls, punched a button. Tony's voice exploded through the room:

"The musical is called *Robin*—Robin being Robin Hood—and if you think the Knicks are incompetent . . ."

Startled, the man hesitated, relaxed his grip on the wire just long enough for me to turn sideways fast and catch a glimpse of him in the bright light from the screen: a man in his fifties with decidedly handsome features, full hair white at the temples, eyes wide, staring at Tony's image.

". . . great tradition of taking from the rich and giving to the poor, the producers of *Robin* . . ."

Tony screamed from the kitchen, long, loud, terrified, and the man's head jerked back almost as if he'd been slapped in the face. She continued to scream. He jumped off me, started for the door, stumbled into the chair I'd fallen over, went down hard, got up and ran out. I could hear him banging down the stairs as I struggled to pull the wire off. He'd twisted it in back and it took all the strength I had left in me to pull it away just enough to breathe freely again.

I could see Tony's silhouette in the kitchen doorway as I got up. I felt dizzy, my legs wouldn't work, and I fell to one knee. She walked over quickly, turned on a lamp, said something I couldn't hear because of the television. I turned it off, looked up at her. Her face was sheet-white and she was visibly shaking.

"Are you all right?" she asked.

"I think so." My voice came out like a whisper. I held my throat, tried again. "I'm not sure."

"Here, wait a minute." She went behind me, looked at

the wire. "Hold onto it, hold it away." She twisted the ends apart slowly, removed it, then helped me up.

We both looked around for my glasses. The place was a real mess. I found them near the front door. After closing the door and snapping the double lock, we both sat down. And, from that point on, Tony started acting strangely. It wasn't just fear or shock or fatigue, although I'm certain she felt all those things. It was something else. A subtle coldness seemed to come over her. Nothing really tangible at first, but I could sense it in her eyes and voice and attitude. I didn't say anything about it because I didn't want to explore it at that point. I was just simply exhausted. But it was there, and it was building.

"Did you see him?" she asked.

"Yes. An older guy, about—"

"You didn't have your glasses on."

"I saw enough. I was so close I didn't need glasses. Whoever he was, that's who killed Long."

She nodded. "He's convinced you witnessed it."

"He's desperate now. He'll try again."

Her voice changed. "And whose fault is that? If you hadn't gone around pretending you knew more than you did—"

"I only did that with you, Tony." I stood, walked slowly to the phone, picked it up. "I better call the cops and get it over with."

She got up quickly. "No. Wait."

I studied her face, hung up the receiver. "You don't have to get involved. You can be gone by the time—"

"That's not it. You're in danger, Daryll. You can't stay here."

"This is my home. I'm tired of running. I'm tired of lying."

"Then *stay!* Stay and be killed. You know all the answers, as usual. Nobody can tell you anything."

"That's not true."

"Don't tell me what's true. You wouldn't know truth if it hit you in the face. You don't want truth, it's too hard, it's too painful. But I'm going to give you a piece of truth anyway, so get ready for it. Know why I wanted to see you tonight? I wanted to say goodbye. Didn't know how to say it to you. No, that's a lie. I knew how. I just didn't have the guts to say it, that's all. Believe that? Didn't have the guts. Well, now I've said it."

"You don't mean that, Tony, I know you don't."

She walked to the door, snapped the lock, opened it, paused with her back to me. "See what I mean? You don't want truth. You don't even believe it when you hear it. Goodbye."

But after she'd left and I'd had a chance to calm down and think about it, I knew something was missing. Something strange was going on. I'd started to tell her what the killer looked like and she'd interrupted me immediately. Why? Why didn't she want to know? I'd started to call the police and she'd stopped me immediately. Why? If she'd just wanted to say goodbye, why had she taken me to her parents' apartment to do it? If she'd just wanted to say goodbye, why had she come all the way home with me? Maybe she was right when she said I wouldn't know the truth if it hit me in the face. Maybe I wouldn't.

But I know lies. You might say I'm an expert on lies.

They've been constant companions all my life.

16

THAT NIGHT I DREAMED that someone was down in the lobby ringing my doorbell. It kept ringing and ringing in a fast staccato, as if someone was desperate to get in. I was in the kitchen in the dark and I couldn't find the buzzer you push to open the lobby door. My hands were groping all over the kitchen walls, but I couldn't find it. I was sweating. The bell kept ringing in crazy, disconnected spurts. I became frantic. Someone I knew was in serious trouble down there, an emergency, and couldn't get in. I threw open my apartment door and ran down the stairs. I saw the lobby door. The window in the door was clear glass, but I couldn't see anyone out there. I reached out for the door handle and turned it. It was locked from the outside. I didn't have the key, but I kept turning the knob and pulling on it with all my strength. I was out of breath and my heart was throbbing. I could hear the doorbell ringing from upstairs. I looked out the window in the door. The lobby was completely empty.

I woke up sweating. The doorbell was actually ringing in a crazy staccato. I sat up quickly. My neck felt swollen and sore as hell. My left arm was stiff and throbbing. I put on my glasses, got out of bed fast. My whole body ached, I felt dizzy, lost my balance, banged into furniture as I ran into the kitchen. I went directly to the squawk box on the wall, pressed the lever, talked into the mike.

"Hello! Who is it?"

The bell stopped. I released the lever, listened for a reply. Silence, then a little static. The bell started again.

"Hello! Can you hear me? Hello!"

The bell stopped. I listened carefully. Silence.

"What apartment do you want?"

The bell blasted away again, long and short bursts, as if the person was in a panic.

I grabbed my keys from the counter, shot back to the bedroom, slipped on my jeans, picked up a shirt and put it on as I opened the door and ran downstairs. I was either rocky as hell or still half asleep, because I remember getting my key ready to open the door; it's never locked on the inside. Before I got to the bottom step, I glanced at the clear glass window in the door. Nobody was there. That stopped me for a moment. I walked up to the door slowly, looked through the glass. The lobby appeared empty. I couldn't hear the bell anymore, but I'd closed my door upstairs. I took a deep breath and opened the door. Sitting directly in front of the door, beneath the window, was my father in his wheelchair.

One glance and I knew he'd been drunk for days. He certainly hadn't shaved for days, his eyes were bloodshot, his hair was a mess. He looked up at me and grinned. He held a pint bottle in his lap.

"Dad, my God, what happened, what's—"

"Thought I'd come to town and get laid."

"How'd you get here?"

"Hitchhiked."

"Bullshit." I smiled, held the door open wide.

He wheeled himself in. "It's the God's honest truth, these kids came along in a yellow VW bus—"

"Bullshit."

As soon as I closed the door, he began crying. His shoulders shook with it and he kept his head down. I remember his shirt, one of his best, was wrinkled and open halfway to his stomach, his underwear shirt was dirty, and his best brown plaid blazer had obviously been slept in. In the buttonhole of his lapel was his master mechanic pin with the sharp black silhouette of a jetliner against a white background, looking almost as bright and shiny as the day he'd received it. I'd only seen him cry on a couple of occasions before. It really tore me up. I didn't know what to say to him.

"Oh, Dad. Don't. Please don't."

"Screw you. I didn't come here to do what *you* want.

Came here to do what *I* want for a change. I've had it. Know what? I'm unhappy. Not happy. Zero happy. I'm getting old, bald and hemorrhoid."

"Come on, I'll take you up."

He worked himself forward in the chair as I lifted his legs slightly and flipped up the steel footrests. Then I turned my back to him, squatted down, got a firm grip behind his knees. He put his arms around my neck, held tight as I stood up. He was very heavy. I kicked the chair out of the way before starting up the stairs. I took them slowly. He leaned his head against mine, began crying quietly again.

"Hey, Daryll. I used to carry you in my arms like this. Remember?"

"No, I guess I was too young."

"I did. Just like this. My boy."

"Don't cry, Dad."

"Why not? Didn't come here to laugh. Came here to cry."

"I thought you came to get laid."

"That's a laugh."

I stumbled on a step, felt him straighten up.

"What happened to your neck?"

"Nothing."

"Nothing. 'Where you going?' 'Out.' Kids. Never change."

"Somebody tried to strangle me."

"Now that's more like it. That I can believe. Somebody tried to wring your neck on you. Good. Just what you need. That's what *I* should've done."

"Why didn't you?"

"Don't know. Didn't know what to do. Like Karl Malden says, 'What will you do? What *will* you do?' Nobody knows till it's too late."

It took a lot of sweat, but I finally managed to get him into the apartment and sitting on the couch. I was out of breath and hurting. The guy weighed a ton. When he took the pint bottle of bourbon out of his pocket, I got him a glass and he had a couple of good belts. I took two aspirin, then poured us a couple of beers and we talked.

"Is this three-point-two beer?" he asked.

"No, it's regular."

He belched, wiped his eyes. "It belches like three-point-two. Your mother hates me."

"No, she doesn't."

"I can't blame her. I'm a three-point-two man. She—she won't make love to me."

"That's because you get drunk as hell every time you—"

"I have to get drunk. If I'm sober, I think about these—" He pounded a fist on his legs. "She used to adore me. Not like. Not love. Adore. You don't forget that. The marriage counselor says we can learn to love each other again. And I ask him: What about adore? And he looks at me like he's never heard that word before in his life."

I nodded. "How long you been going to him?"

"Too long. Where's Ralph?"

I sipped the beer, felt the threat of tears. "He—died, Dad. He died last night."

"What happened?"

I looked toward the bedroom. "It's—complicated. I'll have to bury him this morning. I've got problems, too. You're not the only one with problems."

"Problems? What kind of problems you talking about? You're young, you got a job, you got—"

The telephone rang and I was glad for the interruption. I remember my arm was throbbing as I walked to the phone and I knew I'd have to get over to Bellevue as soon as possible. I'd been too exhausted to do it last night and I knew I was risking an infection.

"Hello."

"Daryll."

"Tony!"

"My parents would like to . . . see you."

"Your parents?"

"Right."

"To check me out?"

"Yes, something like that."

"Just say where and when and I'll be there."

"They'd like to see you tonight, but I know you have to work."

"No, I planned to call in sick. I've got to get over to Bellevue for this arm."

"You didn't do it yet? Christ, Daryll!"

"I'm going to do it right now. Where and when tonight?"

"My parents' apartment. How about—eight-thirty okay?"

"Fine. Beautiful."

"Get over to Bellevue right now. Please!"

"On my way. See you tonight."

When I hung up, I felt excited as hell, but I paused with my hand on the phone. Some of the questions I'd asked myself last night came back. Then I thought: Are you kidding? That's not important any more. Not now. What's important is that she called. What's important is that she'd changed her mind. That she'd obviously given it a lot of thought and talked with her parents about me and wanted them to meet me. That's what was important. What more did I want? If that wasn't proof positive that she was finally getting serious about me, I didn't know what the hell was.

Dad and I talked for a while longer, but I couldn't concentrate and the beer was starting to make him sleepy. He didn't look like he'd slept in some time. He agreed to take a nap. I carried him into the bedroom, helped him get undressed, and hung up his things. I closed the blinds and pulled the curtains and he was asleep within half an hour.

By that time, I'd had a shower, shaved, dressed, and was ready to go. I called the veterinarian on Sixth Avenue I'd used since Ralph was a puppy, explained what had happened, and asked him how to go about burial. He said he'd handle everything, told me to wrap the body in plastic, place it in a box and bring it over.

I did. I did it as quickly as possible. I placed the box under my arm and walked to his office and gave it to him. He explained that the standard procedure was cremation, and he recommended that. I'd never given a moment of thought to what I'd do when Ralph died. I'd heard about pet cemeteries, so I asked the vet about that. He shook his head. I'd always trusted his judgment. He was a good man and I liked the guy. There was no nonsense about him and yet he'd never treated Ralph coldly, he was as personable as they came. He didn't pump me for more details about the death than necessary, but he examined Ralph in another room, came back and assured me he wasn't carrying rabies. He took the bandages off my arm and examined the wounds carefully. The area around them was red and a little swollen. I told him I was on my way to the hospital. He put clean dressings on, said it didn't look like it was infected, but suggested I get over there quickly and have tests.

When I was walking home, I tried to remember Ralph the way he was, but my mind kept returning to the breathless little cries he'd made and the way he'd looked at me, asking for help. At least I knew he hadn't suffered much. It was hard to realize he wouldn't be there waiting to play when I got back. I cried openly on the street and I wasn't ashamed of doing that.

Dad was still asleep when I got home. I called George Fox, explained that I'd been bitten by a dog, that I was on my way to Bellevue Emergency for tests, and that I wouldn't be able to work that night. Instead of being pissed off, he asked if I needed a lift to the hospital. He was like that. He also cheered me up when he said he'd hired a replacement for Aldo. The guy was scheduled for his physical exam that afternoon and would report for work Wednesday evening. No more working the night shift alone. I told him if my tests were okay I'd be there Wednesday even if I had the arm in a sling. I meant it, too. Fox was the kind of boss you'd go the extra mile for. He understood.

I drove the cycle straight over to Bellevue then. One of the women interns did a workup on me, played twenty questions as she examined the arm, called the vet, got a rundown on his findings, took a large sample of my blood, the whole shot. I remember her name, Dr. Powell. Damn good-looking brunette, young, serious, very bright. Had traces of a Southern accent on certain words. I asked her where she was from, just to make conversation. She gave me this look.

"Memphis," she said.

"Nice place, Memphis."

"Ever live there?"

"Just passed through."

"Like shit through a goose, right?"

"Didn't Tennessee Williams live in Memphis?"

"Matter of fact, he did for a while. He had grandparents in Memphis. What happened to your neck?"

"Too much starch in my collar."

She studied it, touched several places. "That hurt?"

"A little." I looked at the nameplate on the breast pocket of her white jacket: DR. C. POWELL. "What's the C stand for? Cat?"

"You've got some ugly bruises here. What happened?"

"What's the C stand for? Curious?"

"Chel."

"Chel. Chel as in Chellie?"

"No. Chel as in Chel we cut this adolescent *shit!*"

I laughed softly. "Somebody tried to strangle me."

"What was used, a wire?"

"Yes."

She jotted it down on her clipboard thing. No change in her expression, no comment, nothing. I had to smile at that. I guess when you work the emergency ward at Bellevue long enough, stuff like attempted murder gets to be routine. Anyway, she gave me a shot of penicillin in the ass, bandaged my arm, wrote out an appointment card to report to the clinic Wednesday afternoon for the results of the blood and urine tests and another check of the wounds. Before I left, I thanked her, smiled, and paraphrased the famous last line of Blanche from *Streetcar:* "Whoever you are, I've always depended on the kindness of black-eyed peas." She told me to kiss her chitlings.

I got back to the apartment about five-fifteen and carried Dad's wheelchair up from the lobby. He was awake and sitting up in bed. We talked for a while and I told him he was welcome to stay as long as he wanted, but I suggested that he call Mother just to let her know where he was. I got out my best suit and was starting to dress when the telephone rang.

"Hello."

"Hello, Mr. Deever?"

"Yes."

"This is Tony's father."

"Oh, yes, sir. I'm looking forward to meeting you."

"Yes, I look forward to it myself, but I'm afraid I have conflicting appointments. It would be much more convenient if we met somewhere else."

"All right, sir. Anywhere you say."

"Have you paper and pencil?"

"Sure have. Go ahead."

"The address is 175 West Eighty-ninth Street."

"Fine. What time would be convenient for you?"

"Would eight o'clock be all right?"

"Sure. No problem. I think I should warn you, I'm crazy about your daughter."

He laughed quietly. "You have very good taste, Mr. Deever. I look forward with pleasure to meeting you. Goodbye."

When I put the phone down, I glanced quickly at the address I'd written. For just an instant, it looked vaguely familiar. Then my father called out from the bedroom, asking me to help him into the wheelchair, and whatever memory the address had triggered was gone.

17

WHEN I REMEMBERED, I was already halfway there, on Eighth Avenue at about Forty-third, and my common sense told me to stop and call the man. Either he'd made a mistake or I hadn't heard him correctly. He'd given me the address of the Claremont Riding Academy. I glanced at my watch. Almost seven forty-five. He'd have left by then, if he'd made the call from his apartment, and of course I didn't even know that. I tried to remember his exact words. His voice had a definite Russian accent, which hadn't surprised me, but I thought maybe that's where the problem was. Still, I was almost positive he'd said 175. Christ, maybe he'd said *East* Eighty-ninth. Or meant to. Or maybe I just assumed it was West because they lived on the West Side. I started to swear out loud and my voice sounded weird inside the plastic visor and helmet. What a terrific first impression on her father, going to the wrong address. "Tony, what kind of clown is *this* you bring us?" Okay, I tried to calm down and think logically. He'd called at about five-thirty. Claremont was open until six-thirty on weekdays. He could've called me from there. Tony was a regular at Claremont; Mr. Sokolow probably was too. Then it occurred to me that he might very well be a director of the riding academy or an owner or maybe even the landlord. God knows, he was wealthy enough. It all seemed to make sense then. I'd heard him correctly, I just hadn't been thinking. He'd mentioned conflicting appointments; obviously, he had a business meeting at Claremont.

At Columbus Circle, I took Broadway and increased my speed a little. I felt confident again. I had plenty of time, I was wearing my best suit, a dark-blue three-piece job, a clean white shirt, a dark tie, and I'd given my best boots a shine. My father said I looked like I was going to a funeral, but you should've seen his eyes when he said it. He was so proud of me that his eyes actually filled. You know Irishmen.

I hung a right off Broadway into Eighty-sixth, then a left into Amsterdam, and found a parking space near the corner of Amsterdam and Eighty-ninth. When I shut off the engine, it was almost eight, maybe a minute to go. I locked my rear wheel, then put my helmet and gloves in the trunk and locked it. I used my curbside mirror to comb my hair and straighten my tie, then walked toward the academy. Eighty-ninth Street was relatively quiet that time of night, a few cars and taxis passing. Streetlights framed trees in pale yellow and threw bright ribbons on the tops of cars. Lighted windows in the old apartment buildings were like yellow slits in the night.

I remember I was on the north side of the street, the same side as the Claremont Riding Academy, so I didn't see the entrance until I was about thirty yards away. The big garage-type rolling door was down and padlocked. Although the windows of the second-floor stable were all open, they were all dark. I experienced a sudden mixture of feelings, but the predominant one was frustration. I glanced at the parked cars nearby. From what I could see, they looked empty. I stopped in front and looked up and down the sidewalk. Nobody in sight except a man about a block away, walking in my direction from Columbus Avenue. I couldn't see his face from that distance, but I kept my eyes on him and listened to his footsteps. His hair appeared full, he wore a suit and tie, and he seemed to be of average height and build.

An instant before he passed under the streetlight half a block away, I caught a quick glimpse of his face. It was the killer. I turned to run and was startled to see a woman approaching quickly, silently, wearing a dark outfit and some type of rubber-soled shoes. She quickened her pace, started to open her purse. My eye caught the fire-escape ladder leading to the second floor of the stable. I broke into a running jump, grabbed the bottom rung, and the ladder pulled down immediately, hit the sidewalk with a sharp clang. I ran up that thing as fast as I could move, heard an almost simultaneous gunshot blast behind me and ricochet above. I made it to the first landing and I'd almost reached the open window when a shot from the opposite direction hit the calf of my left leg and knocked me down instantly. I scrambled through the window, fell to the floor, grabbed my leg. The whole area from the knee to the ankle felt like it was on fire.

Light from the windows illuminated the dark figures of many horses. They'd been upset by the gunshots and were neighing and clomping in place. Their hooves sounded hollow on the wooden floor. There was a heavy smell of leather and manure. I heard rhythmic sounds on the fire-escape ladder, got up quickly, limped toward the horses, felt my way past three or four, patted them, heard them snort and champ. They seemed to be lined up at long, narrow troughs with their halters tied to individual posts. I looked over the backs of several horses and saw the silhouette of the killer squatting on the landing just outside the window. He seemed to be looking down at the woman. Seconds later I heard two rapid gunshots from below and the whine of ricochets off metal. All the horses were spooked badly then, whinnying, rearing, pulling against their halters. When I got another look at the window, the killer was crouched inside, hesitating, not knowing if the horses were loose. There was a loud metallic sound from below as the door was rolled up. I moved quickly down the line of horses, under their necks where I couldn't be kicked, and started untying the halters. The horses peeled off, began running wildly. There were about ten horses at each trough, and I'd untied at least fifteen before the first-floor lights came on, throwing a bright shaft of light up the open ramp. One of the loose horses trotted to the ramp, walked down slowly. Another followed, then a third.

I could see the killer moving cautiously in my direction, gun in hand. The horses were making such a racket by then I didn't think he had a clue where I was. I was right. When he heard something to his right, he turned quickly, walked in that direction. At that point, I began acting on instinct. I continued untying the halters in the second line, but when I moved to the third, I just walked under their necks, advancing toward the approximate spot where we'd converge if he kept walking at the same deliberate pace. I don't remember having any specific plan in mind, I simply knew I'd have to attack him if I was going to stay alive. In those moments, I don't recall feeling any significant pain in my leg, although I was limping. I recall being out of breath, feeling dizzy, and wanting to live. When I reached the end of that line, I saw him in the aisle off to my right, advancing toward me slowly, just the left-side silhouette, his left hand out to fend off the horses, right hand in, holding the gun. I backed up, mounted the next-to-last horse in the line, leaned over his neck to untie the halter. The horse bolted back suddenly. I held onto its neck, kicked its ribs with my right heel. It reared, spun to its right, broke into the aisle and straight toward the man.

At the last second he jumped to his right. I leaped off, heard the gun fire as I plowed into his shoulder. Then we were on the floor and all I remember clearly is grabbing his right wrist with both hands and holding on. He kept chopping at me with the side of his left hand, karate-type shots to my ribs and neck. We were in the aisle, of course, and loose horses were running past, some stumbling on us, others jumping over. Quickly, inevitably, one of them galloped over us. I felt only one hoof, right in my lower back, but he must've caught one in his right shoulder or arm, because he screamed like hell, rolled over so fast that I lost my hold on his wrist. When he jumped to his feet, holding his arm, the gun was gone. I had to roll fast to avoid another horse. I glanced at the floor as I scrambled up, couldn't see the gun in the dark, knew he couldn't either. We faced each other from opposite sides of the aisle, both crouching and out of breath. I felt a sharp pain in my lower back, and my leg began to burn again. Instead of going for me as I expected, he darted to his left, grabbed something from a pole near the trough. It was a bridle. He wrapped it around his left hand, snapped it like a whip, started toward me. He got brushed back by a passing horse, started again.

I turned and tried to run, but I was limping badly. I slammed into the side of a horse in the dark, bounced off, grabbed the halter of another horse, skipped around to its side, swung my right leg up, didn't make it, came down hard on my left leg. The pain was so intense that it really infuriated me. I clawed at the horse's mane, gripped it with both hands, swung the right leg up again and made it. The man was close enough to swing the bridle at me then, missed and hit the horse on the loin. The horse took off, headed for the lighted ramp. He balked at the top, reared, bucked and threw me off sideways. I hit the ramp hard, rolled several times, stopped on my back and saw the killer sprinting down after me. I didn't have time to get up before he was on my back. He looped the bridle over my head, yanked it around my neck and tried to get leverage. For the second time in less than twenty-four hours, a fast image of Long's face flashed into my mind. I reached up and got the fingers of both hands under the leather strap, began pulling, kicking, turning, struggling with a tremendous burst of energy.

The man stopped suddenly, stood up, ran toward the woman and shouted, "Give me the gun!" Instantly, I heard what they'd undoubtedly heard: two sirens in the distance. I glanced at the huge open doorway. At least a dozen people and several horses were clearly visible in the street. Everything seemed to happen with incredible speed then. I remember three horses running past me in quick succession, then galloping toward the door. I couldn't see the killer or the woman. I broke into a limping run for the circular riding area in the rear with the bridle still around my neck. I heard more horses banging down the ramp. By the time I reached the horses in the riding area, the sirens sounded very, very close. I kept running.

I didn't turn until I was against the far wall, well behind the horses. In retrospect, what I saw through that door now seems more like fantasy than reality. Sirens were blaring and red lights flashed on horses backed up at the door. The woman was nowhere in sight, and the killer was fighting his way through the horses, trying to get out. When he did, I lost sight of him because of the horses. I took the bridle off over my head. One siren whined to a stop, then the other, but I heard several more in the distance. I must have decided it was safe, because I started limping past the horses in the riding area and toward the door. I was about halfway there when I heard a single gunshot. I stopped. The horses in the door scattered fast, wildly, some out, some in. People were screaming and shouting in the street. Then the doorway was clear. The red lights pulsated rhythmically on faces in the crowd. Within seconds, the screaming stopped, then the shouting. Then the only sounds I could hear were the sirens in the distance.

As I limped out, I heard the hooves of a horse close behind me. I stood in the doorway. It seemed unreal. Lieutenant Jacobs was on one knee on the sidewalk, leaning over the killer, looking through a wallet. The killer was on his back with one leg twisted under him. He looked dead. Lieutenant Black was standing over them. He asked Jacobs a question. Jacobs just shook his head.

I remember feeling dizzy. I glanced at the faces in the crowd, all bathed in the flashing red lights. They were all staring at the dead man. Someone was moving toward me from the side. When I turned and saw Tony, I couldn't believe it. She rushed up to me, crying, and I put my arms around her. I didn't know what the hell was happening. I really didn't. I felt numb. I didn't even feel the pain in my leg. Nothing.

Two other squad cars arrived, sirens screaming, red lights flashing, doors opening before the cars stopped. Cops jumped out, took a fast look, started shoving people back. The radio was on in both cars, and a woman's voice was dispatching cops to Seventy-second and Lexington in a calm monotone.

Tony spoke softly. "What're you going to tell the police?"

"Everything," I heard my voice say.

"You don't know everything. But you must tell them what you know. When it's all over, I want you to come to my parents' place. They've got a lot of explaining to do. So have I."

"I've got to get to a hospital, Tony."

"What?"

We both looked down. Blood had soaked through my dark-blue trouser leg, which just looked wet, but it was running down the side of my boot now to form a small pool of red on the sidewalk. When I saw it, I felt a dizzy, prickling sensation.

"How bad is it? Can you walk?"

"Yes."

She ran over to Jacobs and Black, began talking and pointing at me. They glanced over and nodded. Two uniformed cops placed a plastic stretcher on the sidewalk next to the dead man, slipped metal poles into its sides, lifted him onto it. They covered his body with a blanket and pulled it over his face.

I didn't even know his name.

18

"EVERY MAN'S WORK . . . is always a portrait of himself." It was true of Mr. Long, whose life was a blueprint of deceit and corruption; it was true of his killer, who played moral arithmetic with people's lives; it was true of Mr. and Mrs. Sokolow, whose lives were haunted by the horror of their past; it was true of Tony, whose values were dominated by those of her parents; and it was true of me, because my entire adult life to that point had been crippled by fear. When all the pieces of the puzzle were finally put in place for me, the portraits that emerged were frightening only in the respect that they were damaged so badly by their own fears, real and imagined, and my life has been changed by that knowledge. For better or worse.

First, the easy pieces. When I told Jacobs and Black everything I knew, they weren't surprised in the least. They explained the basics of the case, information they'd already released to the press. Wealthy Jewish groups throughout the country had been channeling money through Long to pay off Russian government officials who had the authority to issue exit visas. Instead of taking cash for his services, Long frequently insisted on jewels, primarily diamonds. According to a confidential informant available to Jacobs and Black, Long was known to be squeezing the Jewish groups, demanding progressively more and more for his services. Eventually, his demands became virtually impossible to meet. When the Jews were unable to raise that kind of capital on a consistent basis, he threatened to expose their entire operation.

The killer was identified as Joseph Levin, fifty-four, of

New York, a career diplomat with the Israeli delegation to the United Nations. Levin had been the "point man," the Jewish group's direct contact with Long. When his most recent negotiations had failed and Long had made the threat of exposure, Levin had killed him. Obviously, Levin had believed I was a witness to the killing, believed it strongly enough to risk his life, but from that point on, Jacobs and Black were dealing with pure speculation. Had Levin actually seen me in the building that night? Had he seen me running away? Or had he been tipped to the possibility? If so, by whom? I told them honestly that I didn't know. But I had my suspicions by then. The last thing I asked Jacobs and Black was how the hell they'd managed to be among the first police to arrive at Claremont. Simple. And complicated. Jacobs had received an anonymous call telling him that Long's killer was there. The call had come at approximately seven fifty-five. The caller had been female.

My father had the answer to that one. At just about that time, he'd buzzed Tony into the apartment, told her about her father's call to change the appointment. She said she'd been with her parents almost all afternoon, they were home now, and her father hadn't changed anything. She'd wanted to brief me before the meeting. When Dad showed her the address I'd written, she called Lieutenant Jacobs immediately, then ran out.

I wasn't given the key pieces until the following Saturday afternoon, when Tony invited me to her parents' apartment. I remember I was still limping, of course, but relatively little damage had been done. The bullet had entered and exited the fleshy part of the left calf without touching the tibia or fibula bones, and the wounds had required a total of only eight stitches.

The meeting was very low-key at first, and Mr. Sokolow did most of the talking. He appeared to be in his late fifties, a handsome man, slim, balding, and he looked directly into your eyes, like Tony. His ascot was worn loose under a sport shirt and blue velvet blazer. Although his voice had a decidedly Russian accent, it held a great deal more resonance than the voice I'd heard on the phone, obviously that of Joseph Levin.

"Mr. Deever, allow me to explain something. As long as

there are Jews who are held in bondage, and as long as we can do something about it, we will. These days, money can buy freedom. It is the irony of our time that we, people without a country for so long, have come to have so many countries. Russia gave us life. America gave us hope. And Israel gave us a reason to live. What Joseph Levin did, what we did, was and is illegal, but never immoral. And the work must continue. As Joseph himself said so often, 'We can be disappointed if we fail, but we will be doomed if we do not try.' He tried. We will keep on trying." He glanced at his wife, then at Tony, before lowering his head.

Mrs. Sokolow was sipping tea. A slim woman in her early fifties, she looked elegant in a dark shantung dressing gown and would have borne a striking resemblance to Tony except for her hair, blond, worn relatively short, the coloring difficult to detect. She placed her teacup carefully in the saucer before looking at me. Her voice was quiet with fragile overtones of Russian. "Mr. Long was an evil man, Mr. Deever. He deserved to die."

"Yes," Tony said. "But he had his revenge. He made a murderer out of Joseph." She looked at me. "Remember Monday night in front of your building when I met you just after work?"

"Yes."

"And you said something like—I think you said it reminded you of one of those 'there's another guy' scenes? And you asked if he was—I don't know, handsome and rich?"

"Yes. A guy who couldn't possibly lose."

She glanced at her parents, then at me. "This is difficult to explain, Daryll. I was talking about Joseph Levin. We'd been seeing each other for—I think it was close to fifteen months. We weren't engaged, but it was very serious."

In the silence, I just looked at her.

"I swear to God, Daryll, I didn't know. I didn't know until that night at your apartment."

I tried to say something, couldn't.

"I saw him that night. When he tried to kill you. I saw his *face* and I—simply couldn't *believe* it. I had absolutely no *idea* until that night. I swear to *God*."

Her father nodded. "That is the truth. Tonya was never told."

I turned to him. "But *you* knew?"

"Unfortunately, yes. I tried to talk him out of it. God knows, I tried. Joseph said you could identify him. He said the work was too important to jeopardize. Mr. Long's death left a vacuum. There were six people who had committed themselves to escaping. They were known. Joseph needed time to get the money to the Soviet officials. Long was the only contact they knew, so Joseph himself was planning to go over and meet with them."

"We *begged* him," Mrs. Sokolow said. "Begged him to explain it to you, to ask you to forgive him, if you could. And to ask you to remain silent. We told him those six people would surely not want an innocent man's blood on their passports. He wouldn't listen to us. He said it was six lives against one. He said if he failed they would be killed or put in institutions where their minds would be annihilated. Finally, after he attacked you, he agreed with us. Tonya convinced him we should talk with you. He agreed to have Tonya call you and invite you here. He didn't want to be here himself, but he agreed the three of us should go ahead and explain and beg you to be silent."

In the pause, Tony lit a cigarette. "After I called you, I decided I'd better brief you first. You'd be coming over under a completely false impression. I'd been lying and I was sick of it. I wanted to tell you the truth, alone. You know the rest."

"Who was the woman with him?" I asked.

"An Israeli fanatic."

"What happened to her?"

Tony shrugged.

"She's safe," her father said.

"Why'd Joseph decide to cross you?" I asked Tony. "It would've made so much better sense to talk."

"He was under terrible pressure," her father answered. "That Israeli woman? Tonya calls her fanatic because she does not understand."

"Understand *what?*" Tony snapped.

"Understand what she has *suffered,*" he said. "Understand what her *family* has suffered. You do not *reason* with those people anymore, Tonya. Six lives against one, that was ample reason to kill, believe me. More than ample reason. You do not understand that, do you?"

Tony frowned at him. "I'm—frightened."

"Of me? Tonya . . ."

"Both of you."

Her mother sat forward quickly. "It isn't very pleasant, is it? To know what fear is like. Think of living your whole life that way."

"I don't want to think about it."

"I know," her mother said. "That is a luxury you can indulge in. I cannot. I remember it. Six people are waiting now. I remember waiting myself. Looking at the people around me. Faces like mine, like yours, like your father's. I remember them. I can hear them breathing. I can see their eyes and the fear in them. And I remember, I was a young girl then, I remember pleading with God, trying to make a bargain with him. I didn't want to die a virgin. I wanted to know what it was like to be loved by a man. To know what it was like to give birth to a child. Please, God, wait till then, and then kill me. Let me know what it is like to be a mother . . . for one minute."

She began crying softly, fighting for control. Tony got up fast, sat next to her, embraced her.

"And the same people are waiting again," her mother said.

That night I took Tony to dinner at Karen Roy's restaurant in the Village. It was where we were supposed to have our first formal date, remember? In a way, I'm glad we had to wait, because everything was very different. We were like different people. We had white wine and dined by candlelight and the decor was exquisitely Oriental and Karen was her usual beautiful, charming self. You should've seen the look she gave me when she saw Tony. It made me feel really good. I felt closer to Tony that evening than ever before, than I'd ever imagined I could, even in the fantasies. And I had a few real surprises for her.

"I submitted my resignation yesterday," I told her.

"What?"

"In writing, signed and sealed. It's effective in two weeks. Had to give them time to get a new man. They've been good to me there."

"What's happening?"

"Everything's happening. Everything Aldo and I dreamed about eight years ago in Vietnam. Remember what I told you about Aldo?"

"How could I forget?"

"Okay, we had this dream of opening up our own sporting goods store when we got back to the States. Incredible dream. Had it all worked out to the last detail. Nothing could stop us. Christ, everything stopped us. Eight years of roadblocks. Couldn't raise the capital. We tried every scheme you can imagine and still couldn't do it. Okay, last week Aldo came up with the amount we needed, fifty thousand dollars. Found the ideal situation, an established sporting goods store on Broadway near Ninety-seventh. Owned outright by two older guys who were looking to retire. He talked them into accepting the fifty grand as a down payment. They agreed to carry us for the rest, monthly installments at eight percent interest. The bottom line: He bought it. Stock and all. He *bought* it!"

"Daryll! My God, that's absolutely—"

"Just one catch. Know where he got the fifty grand? Borrowed it from loan sharks. Not just *any* loan sharks. Mob people in Jersey and Brooklyn, two different families. Neither one of them knew the other was in it. That guy, he'd had the balls to lie to each of them. Told each family he already had twenty-five grand saved and only needed another twenty-five to buy the store. So, with that kind of collateral, plus their interest, a mere thirty percent, what'd they have to lose? Twenty-five grand was peanuts to each family anyway."

She shook her head slowly. "I hear tell you only con the mob once."

"You heard right. When they found out, both families went looking for him. It's funny, sometimes it takes a crisis to find out who your friends really are. My father always thought Aldo was a punk. For eight years he's been telling me what a loser Aldo is. When I came home from the hospital Tuesday night and Dad found out I'd actually been shot, he blamed himself. He said if I'd gone to the cops immediately instead of taking his advice and lying about it, nothing would've happened. Said if I'd gotten killed, he would've blamed himself the rest of his life. Tony, the guy sat there and cried. Said he'd screwed up his life and my mother's life and my life. Said he was better off dead. Then I told him about Aldo. He couldn't believe it. I mean, he stopped crying and looked at me with his eyes wide open. He says, '*Aldo* did that?' He says, 'I'll be a son of a *bitch.*' Says, 'If that punk has the guts to put his *life* on the line for that store, I got to hand it to him.' Says, 'That takes real *courage* to do a thing like that.' He says, 'I know *you* believe in that pipe-dream store, but I just never thought Aldo was the kind of guy to put his guts where his mouth is.' Then he looks at me and he says, 'Tell him he's got his fifty grand.' "

Tony nodded, frowned. "Your father's got that kind of money?"

"My father's got that kind of money and more. It's a long story, but his union got him a disability settlement of two hundred thousand dollars when he lost the use of his legs in an accident six years ago. For six years he's been sitting around in his wheelchair feeling sorry for himself, drinking himself into oblivion, wondering what to do with the rest of his life. Anyway, the next morning, Wednesday morning, he gets up, starts wheeling himself around the kitchen, making breakfast, banging pots and pans around, and he says, 'Submit your resignation this Friday, four-eyes, you been a janitor long enough.' He says, 'We're naming the store Deever and Mercer, and it's going to have class, we're going to pump some imagination into it.' I go, 'We?' he says, 'You got a third partner, four-eyes, the money man, the marketing man, the guy with the kind of hard-headed business sense to make a pipe dream come true.' He says, 'Quit limping around here feeling sorry for yourself, get your ass in gear, we got work to do.' After breakfast, he gets on the phone, calls my mother, tells her all about it. He was like a new man, Tony, like he used to be, like I remember him when I was a kid. Now he's got my mother working on a big direct-mail advertising campaign, he's got Aldo working on plans for a big grand-opening sale, you know, an open-house party? Aldo's inviting all the Little League kids from the neighborhood, the high school players and coaches, the American Legion players and coaches, all the company-sponsored softball teams that play in Central Park, he's so excited he doesn't have time to *lie!*"

"When's the opening?"

"Tuesday, July first. Start of the fiscal year, the business year. My last day at the Waring Building is Friday, June twentieth. The next Monday, June twenty-third, I'm going to do something for a friend of mine. Something I believe in with every instinct I have in me. I'm going up to Low Library at Columbia and register for the autumn term in the School of General Studies. I'm not going to pick up where I left off four years ago, I'm going to register as a special student in advanced writing. Two courses, nights: Narrative Nonfiction, Wednesdays, seven to nine; Fiction, Thursdays, seven to nine. Required submissions for each course, four chapters every term. That means that a year from now, I'll have two books maybe half finished. At least eight chapters each. I know nobody can teach you how to write, but they can at least put you on a schedule, they can read your stuff, and they can tell you whether you've got anything. And that's what I want to know. That's what I've got to know."

I remember Tony just sat there, looking at me, blinking, frowning. "And you're doing this for a friend of yours?"

"Yeah. A guy I knew four, five years ago, who wanted to be a writer. He gave up. He dropped out of school. Wound up as a janitor. Sometimes I hardly recognize the guy."

She nodded. "Is that what you really want? To be a writer?"

"I want to find out if I could be, Tony. I want to find out if I've got anything worth saying. I want to find out if I've got the discipline to work all day at the store and then come home and try to write something, anything, that I can live with the next morning. I want to give it my best shot, my very best. Then, if the answer is no, that I just haven't got it, at least I won't recriminate myself for the rest of my life for not trying. I've just decided that I'm going to try, that's all. I'm going to try, and try hard, and keep on trying. Maybe it's a pipe dream. Maybe what I'm trying to do is far beyond my capabilities. But how do you know unless you try? So I'm going to dream the dream. I was afraid to before, but I'm not afraid anymore."

That's what I told Tony that night. And that's what I'm doing. I've written this book faster than I thought I could write anything in my life. It just seemed to write itself, if that makes any sense to you. It would be nice to end it by saying that Tony and I became engaged or married, or at least started living together, but we haven't. We're getting there, I think, but we have a lot of learning to do. Learning about ourselves and about each other. We're very different and we want different things. Our parents and backgrounds are vastly different. But we have important things in common.

For example, that September, Tony entered Juilliard on a full-time basis. She did it on her own; in fact, she didn't even tell her parents until she'd started the first week of classes. She feels that she's ready to study music on an advanced level. Not to become a concert pianist or even a professional, but just to find out something. Since she was a child, she's been told that she had a special gift for music, but she'd never put it to a serious test before. She said she never really had the discipline required or the dedication. She seems to have those things now. In three or four years, she'll have a much better perspective. Best of all, she'll never recriminate herself for not trying. Music is what she loves most in her life. And it's what she does best. So she's following that, wherever it leads her.

I'm no philosopher, but I tend to believe that if you want something badly enough, and you won't give up, anything can happen. Yogi Berra's no philosopher, either. He said something once that's become a standing joke in baseball, but it's the statement of a winner, if I've ever heard one. Yogi said: "It's not over till it's over." I believe that. I'll always believe that. Matter of fact, I've seriously considered approaching the guy to do his biography.

The title intrigues me.

ABOUT THE AUTHOR

John Minahan is the author of nine previous books, including the Doubleday Award novel *A Sudden Silence* and the million-copy best seller *Jeremy*. An alumnus of Cornell, Harvard and Columbia, he is a former staff writer for *Time* magazine and was editor and publisher of *American Way* magazine.

Here's Chance Purdue, "Private Eye Ordinaire," in five capers by Ross Spencer—"the funniest writer being published today." Robert L. Fish

THE DADA CAPER 36293 $1.75

Chance Purdue is a magician in bed, but as a detective he leaves a lot to be desired. Yet, when America is imperiled by the Soviet-inspired DADA conspiracy, he is the only man for the job. There's no stopping Purdue as he blazes a trail of deadpan humor through the back streets and bars of underworld Chicago.

THE REGGIS ARMS CAPER 47092 $1.95

Princess Sonia of Kaleski is missing. And rumor has it that Sonia is now married to an American who was in Chance's army battalion, which just happens to be having a reunion. Chance agrees to help find Princess Sonia—but when he arrives at the reunion he finds a lot of folks he wasn't expecting.

THE STRANGER CITY CAPER 75036 $1.95

Chicago mobster Vito Chericola makes Chance an offer his detective's instincts can't refuse—money—and sends him off to a dusty burg named Stranger City to investigate a minor league baseball team: the Stranger City Strangers. In nothing flat, Chance is up to his ears in baseballs, beautiful babes, and burning questions.

THE ABU WAHAB CAPER 76356 $1.95

Spice Dugan, the daughter of an eccentric millionaire and compulsive gambler, is looking for a fast solution to a very sticky problem, and there is only one person who can tackle it—the indefatigable Chance Purdue. In the hopes of spiritual redemption, Spice's father has purchased a relic of an Arab prophet—a sacred, 1,000-year-old sword. And now the dreaded Desert Sands religious cult is looking to retrieve it.

THE RADISH RIVER CAPER 77248 $1.95

The dreaded international peril, Dr. Ho Ho Ho is looking to have the last laugh on America, with an invading army burrowing straight into Radish River. Chance Purdue is the only private eye who can keep them in the hole—that is, with the help of the provocative CIA operative, Brandy Alexander.

Available wherever paperbacks are sold, or directly from the publisher. Include 50¢ per copy for postage and handling: allow 4-6 weeks for delivery. Avon Books, Mail Order Dept., 224 West 57th St., N.Y., N.Y. 10019.

AVON Paperback

Spencer 2-81 (3-2)